ID0743066

GOOD LEADERS, GOOD SHEPHERDS

Discovering Leadership Principles for Effective Priestly Ministry

By

Dick Lyles
Tim Flanagan
Susan Fowler
Drea Zigarmi

ASCENSION PRESS

West Chester, Pennsylvania

Ascension Press
Post Office Box 1990
West Chester, PA 19380
Orders: (800) 376-0520
www.AscensionPress.com

Cover design: Devin Schadt

Printed in Canada

ISBN: 978-1-932927-92-4

CONTENTS

FOREWORD

Providence has given me a great gift. As a bishop called to lead the Archdiocese for the Military Services, I have not only experienced extraordinary graces in ministry, but also have been blessed to meet countless men and women firsthand who excel in the area of leadership. In serving this unique archdiocese over the past nine years, I have come to see that the Church can benefit greatly by those who excel in this discipline. In short, we need not only good shepherds but good leaders.

For a priest and for a bishop, when I think of what it means to be a good shepherd and a good leader, I am reminded of the words adapted from the Book of Wisdom, that we used to use as part of the introit (the introductory words) of the Latin Mass,

> *"In the midst of the people, he opened his mouth, and the Lord filled him with wisdom and understanding."*

We are servants first and foremost in the midst of the people. We serve by coming to know the flock, loving the flock, and being with the flock. We must know their needs intimately and struggle along with them.

Authentic Catholic leadership happens in the midst of the people. This does not mean simply going with the flow. Leading in the midst of the people means setting the pace and direction, keeping the compass of the flock focused on growing closer to our Lord. Sometimes leadership means being out in front, but often it means next to and with the people. Most importantly, it means never losing touch with the people and their innate goodness.

The late Cardinal Cooke once told me that the biggest challenge in the 60s turbulence was leading all forward together. Like the good shepherd, we cannot leave some behind to go forward but must lead all together. This is a great challenge in the changing times of today as well.

The consequences of poor leadership in ministry are substantial. The lack of authentic Catholic leadership skills can cause many problems, both small and large, from ineffectively-run parish council meetings to a personal gruffness on the part of a parish priest that results in people leaving the Church. As a bishop and one who has spent a significant portion of my priesthood in priestly formation, I know that we must be most attentive to our prayer life, daily Mass, and the breviary to have the strength and courage to answer God's call. I also know that one of the great hindrances to effectively serving the people of God are the very real human and organizational challenges we face. As a Church, we need to give due attention to not only *what* we are preaching, but also *how* we are leading.

This is why I am so pleased to recommend *Good Leaders, Good Shepherds.* Written by committed Catholic leaders, this fictional story of a young priest who finds himself in over his head in a new leadership role serves as both an outstanding instruction on the importance of leadership and a wake-up call to those of us who have been leading for years to re-examine our approaches.

Good Leaders, Good Shepherds is an introduction to a innovative method of leadership, combining five practices of leadership with the five contexts in which we lead. The *Good Leaders, Good Shepherds* model is now in use in dioceses across the United States thanks to the efforts of the Catholic Leadership Institute (CLI), a fifteen-year-old apostolate founded to impart proven leadership skills to pastors, priests, and lay leaders. Their efforts are yielding great results.

Although *Good Leaders, Good Shepherds* is a fictional work, it is actually based on real-life situations and stories observed by the authors. The lead characters in the book are based on real people. "Father Frank" is based on a real priest who faced a daunting task. "Charles and Kate" are based on a couple who have reached the highest levels of secular success and have served as Catholic philanthropists and mentors for several decades. The primary lessons learned in this quick-read are that our talents are gifts we are called to use to the best of our abilities.

The benefits of incorporating the lessons within this book into your life will be manifold: a happier, healthier, and holier life, improved relationships, more vibrant parish communities, and a stronger foundation for leaders to pursue sanctity and preach sanctity to others. The lessons also show that time is short, people possess an inestimable value, and our call to lead as priests, pastors, and lay leaders in the Church is not a calling we should take lightly.

As members of the Catholic Church in these first years of the new millennium, we need works like this if we are going to more fully fulfill our respective missions. As our late Pope John Paul II has said, we need to "be not afraid." In this case, we need to "be not afraid"' of shepherding and leading the flock in the midst of the people, despite the challenges we will face. The world is in need.

Are you ready for the challenge?

—Archbishop Edwin F. O'Brien
Archdiocese for the Military Services, USA
Washington, DC

The Story Begins

The past week at Fatima had been everything for which Father Frank had prayed. His anticipation had been so great that he barely remembered any details of his twenty-hour journey from Colorado to Portugal.

His accommodations at the seminary next to the shrine at Cova da Iria were frugal, which was fine—that was exactly what he expected. The priests and people who worked there had been hospitable and gracious. They were actually warmer and friendlier than he had expected. He concluded that this was in part because he had been named after one of the children of Fatima, and in part because he was an American priest who could speak fluent Spanish, which enabled him to get by in Portuguese. When he spoke Portuguese, he felt like a duck swimming in mud, yet the people seemed to genuinely appreciate his efforts and were always eager to help him paddle through.

Only his mother and his friends in Portugal called him Francisco, which was his true given name. His Hispanic mother had convinced his Irish-American father that Francisco was a perfect name since she had given birth on May 13th–the date of the first apparition of Mary at Fatima. He loved the name and felt a special affinity with Fatima for as long as he could remember. But in the third grade he discovered that if he went by "Frank" instead of Francisco, he would have a lot fewer scraps in the schoolyard.

Celebrating Mass at the Chapel of the Apparitions had been a special thrill. Just standing in the presence of that beautiful statue of Mary–discreetly adorned with the bullet from John Paul II's assassination attempt–made Father Frank feel especially blessed. But to be able to share the Eucharist with people who had traveled from all over the world out of devotion to Our Lady made him feel as if he were fulfilling his calling to its fullest. Saying Mass in the shadow of the Holm oak tree, the very spot where Mary had appeared in her glorious apparitions, caused Father to feel as if there were nothing else he could ever do to satisfy his vows more fully.

But surprisingly to Father Frank, he had discovered another place in Fatima that touched him every bit as deeply, though in a very different way. On the second day of his vacation he had strolled along the Way of the Cross, located some two kilometers from the shrine, and meditated on the Stations. After about an hour, he reached Loca do Cabeco, where the three young shepherds had experienced their first apparition of the Angel of Peace.

The instant he laid eyes on the glistening white statues of the three shepherds kneeling before the angel he became mesmerized. The loveliness of these images, nestled in the utter peacefulness of this rocky hillside, captured his spirit. He felt as though his entire being radiated with an energy so pure that he might vanish if a strong gust of wind were to suddenly arise. He knelt there for more than an hour–devoid of any coherent thought–simply experiencing a joy and peaceful calm unlike any he had ever experienced before. After some time, he returned from his reverie to stroll back down the Way of the Cross and back to the shrine.

One of the most remarkable aspects of the trip was that he had been able to repeat this experience for each of the next few days, something that had never happened to him before.

On his sixth day in Fatima, he joined two fellow priests who had just arrived from America and were staying at the nearby Corona Hotel. He happily played the role of tour guide, introducing them to the wonders of this fabulous place. The two had attended seminary with him, so it was good to get caught up and reminisce about old times while seeing the sights.

The unexpected message came that evening when he returned to his room.

José, the seminary's overseer, met him at the front door the instant he arrived. The man had obviously been anxiously waiting for him.

"Ah, finally," he said, skipping the usual greetings and solicitations. "Father Francisco, I have an important message for you from Monsignor Mulvihill. He said you must call him collect as soon as you get this message, no matter what time of day or night it is. Here is the number."

José handed Father Frank a small piece of paper with a phone number written neatly across the center.

"Did he say why?" Father Frank asked.

"No, Father. He just said it was both urgent and important. That's why I've been looking for you."

"Thanks, José." He followed José to the study where the communal phone was located.

José made sure Father Frank was settled in with phone, paper, and pencil, and then quietly closed the door behind him as he left the cleric alone to place his call.

In a few seconds he had the international operator on the line and gave her the information. As the operator placed the call, Father Frank's thoughts turned to Monsignor Mulvihill. Whatever the Monsignor wanted to talk about must be of the utmost importance or he wouldn't have spent the money for an overseas call, let alone a collect return call. Despite being a diocesan priest who did not take a vow of poverty, Monsignor Mulvihill's simple living style could make a Franciscan monk look like a spendthrift. He was also notoriously meticulous in his daily habits.

Father Frank glanced at his watch: seven in the evening in Fatima, which meant it would be noon in Colorado. Monsignor always said his mid-day prayer at 11:45 a.m. and sat down for lunch precisely at noon. People set their watches by him. And no one dared interfere with his routine. *Oh well*, Father Frank thought. He said to call as soon as I got his message. So if I interrupt his lunch, it's really his fault.

Just as he was beginning to wonder if Monsignor would allow his lunch to be interrupted, the senior cleric's voice resonated from the other end of the line, sounding even more somber than usual.

"Is that you, Father Frank?"

"Yes, Monsignor. Your voice sounds so clear it's like you were right next door rather than halfway around the world."

"I can hear you clearly, too. I'm afraid I have bad news."

An anticipatory knot began to form in Father Frank's stomach. Before he could respond, Monsignor Mulvihill continued. "In the middle of the night, Monsignor Firko had a heart attack and died."

"Monsignor Firko?" Father Frank exclaimed. Firko was pastor of one of the more vibrant parishes in the diocese. The parish hadn't always been that way, however. Most of its current vitality had developed since Monsignor Firko took over as pastor at St. Joseph's parish three years ago. Before then it had been one of the more nondescript parishes in the region.

"Yes. It caught everyone by surprise. He and the Bishop had dinner yesterday and everything seemed fine. When he didn't show up for 7:00 a.m. Mass this morning, several parishioners went looking for him. It appeared he went peacefully."

Father Frank thought, *This will affect a lot of people.* Monsignor Firko had served in several parishes besides St. Joseph's. He had been extremely popular everywhere he went, and he was only in his mid-50s.

"We would have let you know under other circumstances," the Monsignor continued, "but because of the Bishop's decision, I thought I'd better contact you right away."

"Bishop's decision?" Father Frank asked.

"In consultation with the personnel board," Monsignor explained, "he's assigned Father James Manion to fill in for the next 30 days, at which time he wants you to take over as Monsignor's permanent replacement."

Frank liked Father James. He was a dedicated and holy man and always had a smile for everyone. "Why doesn't he make Father James the permanent pastor? He's more experienced, and he relates to people a lot like Monsignor did." He winced as he caught himself already referring to Monsignor Firko in the past tense.

"He's been accepted to study canon law in Rome starting this fall, and the Bishop would not consider abandoning that plan," Mulvihill said.

"But surely there must be someone else better prepared than I am for that job."

"The Bishop and the personnel board have given it quite a bit of thought. It's something that had been in the works for a while. It's been the topic of discussion at the last two meetings of the regional vicars. In fact, at their last meeting they chose you to succeed Monsignor in July anyway, because he had requested an assignment at the university starting in the fall and the Bishop had granted his request. We decided not to raise the issue with you until after your vacation."

"Are you sure?" Father Frank asked. "The last time we talked I understood that I wouldn't become a pastor for at least another year or two."

"I'm sure," Mulvihill replied. "That was six months ago, and a lot has changed during that time."

Father Frank didn't know what else to say. Taking over for Monsignor Firko seemed like an insurmountable challenge. He would have been great at the university. Firko was experienced, popular, and well-liked by everyone. In addition to being a very devout man, Monsignor Firko also brought out a wholesome and energized spirituality in his parishioners. Father Frank felt a huge sense of inadequacy just thinking about how hard it would be to fill his shoes.

"I guess I should try to come back early," Father Frank finally responded.

"No. The Bishop and I discussed it and don't think it's necessary. You'll have your hands full soon enough. Relax for a few more days and we'll see you when you get back." Monsignor paused and then said, "Take a moment to reflect on Exodus, chapter four, verse ten."

"Anything else?" Father Frank said, not knowing off the top of his head the verse Monsignor just mentioned.

"Everything else can wait until you get back."

"Thanks, Monsignor. I'll talk to you later," Father Frank said as he slowly slipped the phone back into its cradle.

When he returned to his room, the young priest slumped solemnly on the edge of his bed, trance-like, as he thought about the future. *I'm not ready for this*, he thought. *I know it's something I've always wanted, but just not yet. Me, a pastor already? What on earth could the Bishop have been thinking?* With slow, robotic movements, Frank grabbed his Bible from the nightstand and slowly turned the pages to chapter four in the Book of Exodus.

He nodded knowingly as his eyes fell upon the forgotten verses:

"But I am not the right person for this job," exclaimed Moses. "Fear not. I shall be with you," responded the Lord.

He slowly closed the book and placed it on the nightstand next to the bed. Every bit as methodically,

Father Frank retrieved his breviary, completed Evening Prayer with as much devotion as he ever had in the past, and tried to get some sleep.

He awakened the next morning more tired than he had been the night before when he had finally and fitfully dozed off. He showered, dressed, said Morning Prayer, and then went to meet his friends for breakfast at the Corona Hotel.

"Hey, Frank," Father Earl Rafferty said as he entered the small dining room. "We were beginning to wonder if the seat we saved for you would be used."

"Sorry I'm late," Frank replied.

"You OK?" Father Dan Busch asked. "You look like you've been through the wringer."

"Didn't sleep too well last night."

"Something happen?" Earl asked.

"Monsignor Mulvihill called to tell me that Monsignor Firko died. It was totally unexpected."

"Oh my. I'm sorry to hear that. He wasn't that old. Had he been sick?" Earl asked.

"No, he wasn't."

"I didn't realize you two were that close."

"I knew him," Frank said, "but we really weren't that close. He was one of the icons of the diocese, a guy everyone respected. And he'd been around a while. I'm just one of the new kids on the block, so I wasn't really on his level."

They both thought about Frank's comment while Sergio, the head of the family that owned the Corona, poured Frank a cup of coffee and placed a basket of rolls in front of him. That's the one thing Frank had trouble adjusting to in Portugal: No one ate breakfast there. All you got was coffee and rolls. You could ask for tea and they would struggle to get it. But that was about it. He had long since decided that the first meal he would devour upon returning to the United States was breakfast–a huge Spanish omelet, hash browns, and toast loaded with strawberry jam–no matter what time of day it was. The rolls were hard and dry, but the coffee made up for them. Brewed rich and strong, it was hard to imagine a better cup anywhere on Earth.

Frank broke the silence. "The reason Monsignor Mulvihill called is that the Bishop wants me to take Monsignor Firko's place as pastor of St. Joseph's."

Dan smiled. "And that's why you look like you just came out on the losing end of a dog fight?"

"I think I understand," Earl said. "I know you're saddened by the loss of Monsignor Firko, as we all are. But are you upset because the Bishop wants you to replace him?"

"He's already made the decision," Frank said.

"I think 'a bit upset' may be an understatement," said Dan. "Unless you mean a bit upset in the same context that Jacob was a bit upset after wrestling with God."

"You're not responsible for the circumstances," Earl added. "It's not your fault Monsignor Firko passed away. You can't possibly feel guilty about it."

"I'm sad about Monsignor Firko and I'll pray for his soul—I and about a million other people who loved him," Frank said. "The problem is that I can't take over for him. They need someone who can do all the things he did to make that parish great. I don't even know where to begin."

"Start with the fact that you're a well-trained priest, devout, and dedicated to your calling," Earl told him. "And as a diocesan priest, a huge part of your calling is to be a pastor."

"Since we were ordained, and especially in the past year or two, I've given that a lot of thought," Frank said. "Our theology training in the seminary was great. It couldn't have been better and I loved every bit of it. Our training in canon law was every bit as good. But recently, as the likelihood of me becoming a pastor has become more imminent, I've been watching a number of the pastors in our diocese, including Monsignor Firko. They're good theologians and all that, but the good ones all had something else. Something else that I don't think I have. Not only don't I have it, I don't even know where to turn to get it."

"What is 'it'?" Dan asked.

"If I knew that, I don't think I'd have this ten-pound knot in my stomach right now."

"Well, how much do we know about 'it'?" Earl asked.

"You watch these guys—take Monsignor Dolan for example. He gets his parishioners really charged up.

They volunteer for things, they bring him great ideas, and they all want to contribute to making the parish great. So everywhere you turn in his parish good things are happening. They're adding on to the school, daily Mass attendance is high—you can't find a parking place within a block of the church for any of five Ash Wednesday Masses they schedule. Compare that to some of the other parishes where people are just going through the motions."

Earl shrugged. "And you don't think you know enough to be able to do what the good ones do?"

"I know I don't know enough," Frank said, as he felt the knot in his stomach grow even larger.

"How do you know?" Earl persisted.

"Because I know me. I get along well enough with people and I generally have fun when I teach classes and do things in the parish. But I'm not good at asking people to do things, I'm not good at responding to confrontation, or handling conflict, and I've never been a 'take charge' kind of guy. In fact, I'm always the shy one who goes along with what other people decide."

"But that doesn't mean you can't be a pastor," Dan said.

"It makes me question whether I can be a good one, though."

"Good people make good pastors," Earl said. "And you're a good person."

"Yeah, well..." Frank nodded. "I think we'd better head on over to Cova da Iria and visit the shrine or all you'll be able to tell people about your visit here was the marathon breakfast you had at the Corona Hotel."

The three priests spent the next few days continuing to be enthralled with the beauty and wonders of Fatima. They prayed regularly and talked only occasionally about Frank's fears. This was in part because Frank didn't want to impose on their visit with his own concerns, and in part because after the first tidal wave of emotion, he had been much better at keeping his fears hidden.

Finally, it came time for Frank to head home. Dan and Earl met him at the seminary and helped carry his bag to the lobby to wait for the taxi that would take him to the bus stop for his ride back to the airport at Lisbon.

"I had an idea last night," Dan said out of nowhere.

"What's that?" Frank and Earl turned their attention to Dan.

"Remember Kate Forrest from the seminary?"

"Sure," Frank said. She was the most devoted of the fifteen members of the seminary advisory board. Kate's husband, Charles, had been a prominent and successful businessman in the high-tech industry. Because of her close ties to his work and her raising three successful kids, she was a veritable mother-lode of practical advice, worldly wisdom, and help in solving a broad assortment of problems.

"I think you should go see her when you get back," Dan said.

Frank looked at him curiously. "Really? Why? What could she do?"

"I don't know exactly," said Dan. "But I think you should go see her anyway. I'm sure she'd have some suggestions and would be able to offer at least a few ideas that would help you through this."

"Maybe I will," said Frank.

The taxi arrived, so they all said their good-byes and Frank embarked on his long journey home.

As Frank's plane taxied to the terminal stateside, his thoughts turned to his own pastor, Monsignor Joe Meeker, who had been kind enough to offer to meet Frank at the airport upon his return. It was typical of the Monsignor's thoughtfulness that he would take time out of his busy schedule to shuttle Frank from the airport to the rectory at St. Mary's.

That's another trait that distinguishes the good ones from the not-so-good, he thought. *The good ones always see that the big, important things get done. But somehow they always manage to have time for the not-so-big things as well, like picking me up at the airport. My previous pastor would never have had time to do this because he was always too busy. But doing what? Most of the big important stuff never got done either. What was it that made the difference?*

Frank quickly disembarked with the other passengers, trekked to the baggage claim area, retrieved his suitcase, and spotted Monsignor Meeker's car at the curb just as the security guard was telling him to keep moving. He tossed his bag in the backseat of the beige SUV and they were off.

During the short drive back to the rectory Frank related the highlights of his trip, including his time with Dan and Earl. In return, he was treated to the news about the happenings at St. Mary's in his absence and learned the details of Monsignor Firko's funeral.

Not once did the topic of Frank's new assignment surface.

That would be typical of Joe Meeker, Frank thought after they had finished Evening Prayer together and he was readying for bed. *He would know it would be an uncomfortable subject for me, even though he probably had significant input into the Bishop's decision. So he wouldn't want to inject anything that might be negative into my homecoming. Just welcome me back and make me feel at home and cared for. There'd be plenty of time to talk about the new assignment later.*

The only reason he slept at all that night was because he was exhausted from his long flight home. But it wasn't a restful sleep. He tossed and turned most of the night, which was uncommon for him. He awoke the next morning again feeling unrested, now far too common an occurrence.

It was Wednesday morning and Father Frank had the 7:00 a.m. Mass, so he quickly got back into the swing of things. Since Monsignor Meeker had the 9:00 a.m. Mass, they weren't able to get together until mid-morning.

"The Bishop tells me you're going to take over as pastor at St. Joseph's," the Monsignor said.

"Unless he comes to his senses and appoints someone capable," Frank replied.

"I don't want to hear any of that talk. You've paid your dues, served your time, so to speak. Now it's time to see what you're really capable of doing. All of us have high expectations."

"Even modest expectations would be overdoing it in my case," Frank insisted.

"Baloney. You keep talking like that, and I'll give you all the early Masses next week. You'll do just fine once you get over your first-time jitters. Don't worry, everyone has them. It's normal. The most important thing is to just get on with it."

"Easy for you to say."

"You'll see," Monsignor said. "Now. We've got to spend the next few days turning over your responsibilities to various lay staff members because it doesn't look like I'm going to get a replacement for a while. I've listed what I think should go to whom. If you agree, then contact them, arrange a meeting and work out how you're going to turn everything over. If you don't agree, then let's talk about it and decide together what to do."

"Will do." The reality of the transfer hit Frank especially hard. Until now it had all just seemed abstract and remote. But this made it real.

Frank returned to his office, went through the list, agreed that it all made sense, and started working through it. He quickly got caught up in the moment and stayed blissfully busy, focusing on the present and not the future for the remainder of the week and through the weekend.

The following Monday was fine, but on Tuesday, Monsignor Meeker's day off, the terror once again caught up with Frank.

He had arisen early, said the early Mass, recited his Morning Prayer, then celebrated the 9:00 a.m. Mass before settling down to breakfast alone when panic struck. Other than celebrating Mass for a couple more weeks, all of his other duties at St. Mary's had been transferred to different people. The next logical step would be to call Father Manion to work out a plan for taking over at St. Joseph's.

But Frank simply couldn't bring himself to make that call. Several times he started and found an excuse to stop. He occupied his time with meaningless tasks and busy work. To put it simply, he was miserable, anxious, and downright scared. He felt virtually paralyzed, overcome with an anxiety so severe he couldn't take even the simplest steps he needed to move his life forward.

He finally went into the sacristy and prayed for an avenue of escape. Just before noon he came to the reluctant conclusion that there would be no way out of his predicament. So he took what to him was the most logical step. He turned it over to God.

He prayed, "Heavenly Father, if this is Your will, then I will respond faithfully to the best of my abilities. My abilities here are limited. I'm not up to this task without Your help. So please, give me the guidance, strength, and wisdom I need to carry out this calling in a way that brings glory and honor to You."

He left the sacristy feeling at peace with his situation, wondering what he should do next. *I guess I'd better call Father Manion*, he thought. *But I don't know what to say or where to start.*

He had only been back in his office for a few seconds when the phone rang.

"Hi, Father Frank. This is Kate Forrest. Remember me?"

"Of course," he replied, although her voice reminded him that he'd completely forgotten Dan's suggestion to call her upon his return from Fatima. "How have you been?"

"Fine, thanks. I'm still enjoying my involvement with the seminary. And I had a special treat this morning when Father Dan Busch called. He said you and he and Father Earl had a great time at Fatima."

"Yes we did. It was good to be able to share the experience with those two."

"He also told me you're taking over for Monsignor Firko. Congratulations."

"Yeah. Thanks, I think."

"Are you still feeling a bit anxious about that?"

"More than a bit."

"How about if we got together to talk about it?" she asked.

"Sure." Frank felt a slight hint of relief.

"Charles and I are going to the ranch tomorrow for a few days. Can you get away and join us? I think he might have some ideas that can help. At the very least, just having someone to talk it over with can't hurt."

"That's a great idea," Frank said. "There's a priest visiting a family in the parish. I'll get him to cover my Masses. I've given all my other duties away, so I don't think Monsignor will mind."

"Great. Then we'll see you tomorrow afternoon."

Hope was a wonderful thing. Although Kate's call didn't provide Frank with specifics, it did offer him hope that somehow he could find some answers that would put his mind at ease and help him to deal with the challenges that lay ahead.

The three-hour drive to Eagle's Nest Ranch was peaceful and pleasant. Late May and early June were some of the most beautiful times of the year in the Rockies. The streams rushed full, fed by the beginnings of the snow melt, and the plants had all surged through their tentative spring blossoms and were on a mad dash for their summer growth splurges.

Frank pulled up to the intercom at the gate just off the highway and pushed the buzzer.

"Is that you, Father Frank?" Kate Forrest's voice crackled through the speaker.

"Yes, it is."

"OK. See you soon." The gate swung slowly open to let him pass. The sound of Kate's voice gave Frank a good feeling. She had always shown a personal interest in every seminarian and frequently invited groups of them either to her house for dinner or to the cabin for a weekend. The Forrests provided the seminarians with what amounted to a home away from home—a place where they could get out into the world, away from the pressures and confines of the seminary and feel comfortable, relaxed, and supported. Kate was a devoted wife and mother of her own small brood of terrific kids. But she had made a special commitment to the seminary and took her role seriously. She was probably closer to many seminarians than most faculty members. In short, the seminarians revered and respected her, and rightfully so.

The drive from the gate to the cabin took about five minutes, winding through several meadows and valleys surrounded by some of the most beautiful mountain country in the world. He passed the fork in the road that split off to where the ranch foreman and some of the staff lived. He finally reached the huge open valley where the cabin stood.

As he entered the valley, which was carpeted with foot-high grass, he noticed the aspen grove nestled against the rock cliff wall off to his right. He knew from previous visits that later on in the day, just before sunset, about forty huge turkey vultures would straggle in from miles around to roost for the night. In the mornings they would fly the short distance from the aspen grove to rock outcroppings or bare tree limbs located in the sunlight. There they would stretch their wings and ruffle their feathers until they were warm enough to rise on the updrafts that caressed the cliff faces and surrounding valley walls. Then they would float gracefully on the wind currents until the day's meal was sighted, after which they would eventually return to the aspen grove. Frank considered it one of nature's most intriguing rituals and he always felt blessed to be able to participate in it, even if only as an observer.

After passing the aspen grove he turned left and pulled into the driveway. It always seemed odd to him that they called their home a cabin. It stood three stories high, and had more than 10,000 square feet of living space. There was an office for Charles, a huge two-story-high dining and living room, a massive kitchen that would make most restaurateurs envious, and an exquisite chapel on the first floor. Whenever a member of the clergy was present, he would celebrate daily Mass there. On the floor below were a game room and full-service wet bar, a fitness room, a theater, a children's playroom, several bathrooms, and doors that opened out onto a spacious patio overlooking the meadow. The uppermost floor had several huge bedrooms with bathrooms, and there were fireplaces everywhere. The entire place was the most tastefully decorated home that Frank had ever seen, even in pictures.

Kate and Charles stepped outside to greet Frank as he pulled to a stop in front of the cabin.

"You look great," she said as she hugged him warmly.

"Thanks," Frank replied. "It's really good to see you both."

"Let's get you settled in and then we want to hear all about your Fatima trip," Charles said.

Soon they had taken Frank's bag to his room and were settled in the breakfast nook with mineral water and snacks, recounting his trip.

Later on they all took a short hike. On their way back, they passed near the aspen grove just as the first few turkey vultures began to settle in for the night.

As the sun set, they celebrated Mass in the chapel and then sat down to dinner.

Charles finally broached the big topic. "Kate tells me you're going to be the new pastor at St. Joseph's."

"That's right," Frank said.

"How does it feel?"

"To be honest, not as good as it should, I guess."

"Why's that?"

"I think I pretty much know how to be a good priest, but I'm not sure I'm at all prepared to be a good pastor. I've seen a lot of great priests who turned out to be not too great at pastoring, and I don't want to be one of them."

"So you don't feel like you've had much training in all the enabling skills that make a parish run effectively?" Charles asked.

Frank shook his head. "Very little."

"They don't offer much in the way of leadership training at the seminary, do they?"

"Or anyplace else. We only had a couple of courses that briefly touched on that subject. No one seemed too interested—even the instructors. And when you talk to other priests, or even bishops, they downplay the whole subject, even though most of them tell me that they spend about two-thirds of their time governing. They just don't think understanding leadership is that important. Do you think it is?"

Charles nodded. "I believe it is way more important than most clergy realize."

"Then why aren't there many priests who agree with you, and why has it been a topic that is so overlooked?"

"I've often wondered the same thing. I think there are a variety of reasons, and I'm not sure any of us know them all. But I think one reason is that there's a feeling our faith and spirituality should always come first, coupled with a fear that if we put too much emphasis on something like leadership skills, some people might lose sight of that fact. Another is that some people think leadership skills are just ways to manipulate people and that if we simply rely on God, then we don't need to even think about things like leadership skills."

"I've been trying to figure out what makes the good pastors and parishes different from the not-so-good," Frank said.

"Any answers yet?"

"I can tell you what *happens* in the good parishes that make them different from the not-so-good ones. They are vibrant Christian communities of worship with strong evangelization, teaching, service, and stewardship. But I can't get a handle on what *causes* those different things to happen. That's what I really need to know."

"I've been volunteering in different dioceses throughout the state for quite a few years now," Charles said. "At the same time I've run a few successful businesses and helped out several volunteer organizations. I can say with a reasonable degree of confidence, based on quite a bit of experience, that the difference is *leadership*—an answer many clerics are reluctant to accept."

"I don't want to sound reluctant, and certainly don't want to seem even the least bit disrespectful," Frank said, "but I'm having trouble seeing it, and I've been really trying to study this whole area."

"I hear you being honest, not reluctant, and I don't think there's a disrespectful bone in your body. I just don't think you can find something—or even see it—if you first don't know what you're looking for."

"What do you mean?"

"Let's start by agreeing on what we're looking for," Charles suggested. "Exactly what is leadership?"

The question caught Frank off guard. His first inclination was to say, *Everybody knows what leadership is,* but he caught himself, knowing that really wasn't an answer.

"I guess I'd have to say it's getting out in front and having people follow you," he finally said.

"Maybe that's another reason clerics shy away from it. A lot of them probably ascribe to that same notion, which sounds a bit prideful and therefore undesirable."

"How would you define it?"

"Let me give you my favorite formal definition and then we can talk about what it means."

"Sounds good to me."

"Formally defined, leadership is the act or process of engaging and satisfying the motives of followers in a context of conflict, competition, or achievement that results in followers' taking action toward a mutually shared vision," Charles said.

Frank held up a hand. "Wait a minute. I want to write that down so I'll remember it."

"Let me get something for you," Kate said.

She gave Frank a pen and pad. Frank then asked Charles to repeat the definition, which he did.

"Now let's relate that to the role of the priest," Charles said, "which is what?"

"As an extension, or representative, of the bishop … to sanctify, educate, and govern the people of God."

"And the role of the pastor?" asked Charles.

He shook his head. "Really no different. The pastor's role is basically the same. To sanctify, educate, and govern within the boundaries of a particular parish."

"So if those are the ends, or goals the pastor is striving for, what are the means—the actions or processes available to the pastor to achieve those goals?"

"Certainly prayer would be one," Frank replied.

"Without a doubt the most important one," Charles nodded. "Then what?"

"I think I see where you're going."

"'Prayer without action' …you know how the saying goes."

"And the actions needed would be the actions you refer to as leadership."

"Exactly," Charles said. "Leadership isn't something a priest would practice instead of prayer or in lieu of faith. It's something a priest or pastor would use to enhance his effectiveness."

"OK," Frank said. "I accept all that. But, again with no disrespect intended, as I look at your definition of leadership, all it does is intimidate me. I mean, if that's what I have to do, then I don't know how to do it."

"That's also the trouble with a lot of the leadership courses that are out there," Charles stated. "They teach students about leadership, or maybe even about how to do it, but they don't make them leaders."

"Can you *teach* people to be leaders? From what I've seen, some people are born with what it takes and others aren't."

"I believe people are born with different levels of leadership potential. Just like they're born with different levels of potential for everything else. You can teach people to draw, but everyone isn't going to turn out to be Van Gogh. Just because they're not going to be the next Van Gogh doesn't mean we shouldn't teach them to draw, if drawing is important to them. There is a certain level of potential everyone can achieve as a leader if they receive the right training. Unfortunately, most people are performing way under their potential because they haven't been trained to develop the potential they do have."

"So although I may never be as great a leader as John Paul II or Benedict XVI it doesn't mean I can't be a good leader in my own right," Frank observed.

"Exactly."

"But where do I go if I want to learn to be a leader instead of just learning more about leadership?"

Charles smiled. "I can help you with that."

Kate had been listening supportively. "But let's not get into it tonight. Let's start fresh tomorrow after you've had a chance to reflect on what you've discussed so far and we've all had a good night's sleep."

"Thanks. I feel as though my prayers are being answered," Frank said.

He fetched his breviary and they prayed together before retiring for the evening. That night he had the best sleep he'd had in weeks.

The next morning they celebrated Mass again and then sat down together for breakfast.

"How did you sleep, Father?" Kate asked.

"Better than I have in a while. It was perfect for getting ready to learn more about leadership ideas."

Charles nodded. "Great."

"So, are you going to give me the secret formula I need to be a leader?"

"That's one myth I'd like to dispel early. If it were easy to do it well, everyone would be a star performer.

Leadership can be learned and mastered, but it takes time and effort."

"Where do we start, then?"

"First we need to understand that leadership is something that is practiced in one of five different contexts."

"What do you mean by 'contexts'?"

"When you talk about the leadership practices or approaches necessary to lead an organization—say a parish, for example—then the first thing to understand is that there are different contexts in which those leadership practices must be carried out. There are five of them: leading self, leading others in a one-to-one context, leading teams or groups, leading the overall organization, and leading alliances, which are the more formalized relationships your parish may maintain with other organizations. Too often, leaders ignore one or more of these contexts or view them from a very fragmented perspective, meaning they don't realize that what they do in one context affects their performance in the others."

Frank took notes fast and furiously as Charles continued.

"Let me illustrate through the use of a simple example. Right now, you are primarily functioning in the *self*-context, because you are focused on how to take charge of your own personal development in the context of your new role as pastor. If you were more focused on your parish council and how well it was performing its role, you would be functioning more in the team context. Or different still, if you were evaluating the performance or directing the efforts of one of your lay staff—your director of religious education, for example—then you'd be functioning in a one-to-one context."

"I see," Frank said.

"But for now let's just focus on the self-context. The context of leading yourself is further sub-divided into two sub-contexts. The first is to understand yourself in preparation for leadership."

"What do you mean by that?" asked Frank.

"Basically it means you should understand how your personality influences the choices you make as a leader," Charles explained. "We all have different personalities. Our personalities make a big difference in how each of us might choose to act in different situations. Only if you have an understanding of yourself can you hope to take charge of yourself and your actions when you deal with others. And by the way, the more you understand yourself, the more you're likely to gain insights into the personality traits of others in ways that will make you more effective in dealing with them."

"So the better I understand my *self*, the better I should be able to lead in all five contexts, and not just the self-context," Frank said.

Charles smiled. "You got it."

"OK, so understanding myself in preparation for leadership is the first sub-context of leading self. What's the second?"

"The second sub-context of leading self is more role-related. For example, for you it means to know what you want to accomplish as a pastor, and then being able to demonstrate the skills and behaviors necessary for planning and organizing personal priorities, taking charge of self-development, and accomplishing short- and long-term personal goals in that role."

"The one thing you haven't mentioned in either of the two sub-contexts is spirituality," Frank said.

"That's because your spirituality is at the core of everything you do. Without solidly grounded spirituality, then all is naught. But I don't think spiritual formation is your greatest challenge here."

"It's not, although it's always a top priority and something I need to work on all the time."

"We all do," Charles said. "But I've found most priests are reasonably diligent at attending to their spiritual formation. Unless, of course, they get so overwhelmed by the demands and pressures of their pastoral duties that they let it slip."

"I've seen that happen," Frank nodded. "And although self-leadership–perhaps all leadership–may not focus directly on spiritual formation, I can see that if I do the leadership piece of it right, then I should have more time and energy set aside to maintain my spiritual formation properly."

"I've seen that happen a lot."

"Let me make sure I've got what we've talked about so far," Frank said. "At the core of everything is my spirituality. My leadership practices in my role as pastor shouldn't interfere with either my spirituality or my spiritual formation. In fact, each should help strengthen the other. My spirituality should help me to become a servant leader in the image of Jesus, and if properly applied, my leadership practices should enhance my spirituality."

"Right on." Charles gave him a thumbs-up.

"Then surrounding my spirituality, which is the core, is an understanding of my self."

"Yes," Charles said. "Keep going."

"Once I understand my core spirituality and personality, then I have to know what I want to accomplish as a pastor and be able to do the necessary planning and personal goal-setting that will take me in that direction. But I also need to take charge of my own self-development so I can learn and grow as I move toward those goals."

"You must have been at the top of your class in the seminary. You didn't miss a thing. And your insights are right on."

Frank blushed. He wasn't the greatest at accepting compliments. "It does make sense when you think about it," he said. "What's next?"

"Next I think we take a break. I have a few phone calls to make, and I think it would be helpful for you to reflect for a while on how you're going to apply this knowledge. The knowledge itself isn't valuable unless you do something with it. It's a beautiful day outdoors, so we might as well take advantage of it. Why don't you head on over toward Inspiration Point and I'll catch up with you later? Do you remember how to get there?"

"I do," Frank said. "And thanks."

As Frank crossed the meadow and made his way toward the trail that led to Inspiration Point, he sensed energy and excitement everywhere. His feet couldn't have felt any lighter than if his hiking boots had been house slippers. He almost skipped up the trail to the meadow where beavers maintained a dam on Cottonwood Creek.

He slowed down before reaching the meadow and tiptoed up the trail, hoping to catch a glimpse of the beavers. He crept slowly around the last curve in the trail and, sure enough, three beavers were busily working on the dam. Two gnawed at aspen saplings a few yards from the creek and the other sat atop the dam, rearranging some of the structure with the newly gnawed branches. He watched them for a while, in awe of their efforts.

Finally he moved toward the dam. In an instant the beaver on top slid into the water, slapped the surface with its paddle-like tail and disappeared. Upon hearing the loud slap the other beavers quickly scurried into the pond and disappeared below. They would huddle inside the dam until the intruder was long gone.

Frank strolled over to the pond, captivated by its beauty and tranquility. The sound the water made as it trickled over the dam was like music—God's music, which had graced these mountains long before people ever disrupted the routine of these beautiful creatures.

He knelt down at the edge of the pond to get a closer look. As he did, he was surprised to notice that the pond reflected his image. It gave him an eerie feeling. The image was clear, yet textured by the water and the shallow bottom of the pond, even though the surface was as smooth as glass. The more he studied his reflected image, the more it moved him.

An old saying he'd heard years ago but had long forgotten entered his thoughts: *God's gift to you is your potential. What you do with it is your gift to God.* It had been quite a while since he'd allowed himself to consider the notion that he might have the potential to be a good pastor.

As a high school student he had always assumed he would someday be a pastor, although back then it was unlikely he made a distinction in his mind between being a priest and a pastor. That distinction didn't enter his mind until the final summer of his diaconate, which he spent at a parish that had a lethargic and unpopular pastor. It was Frank's first experience with a pastor who created animosity and negativity in his parish. Until then, he had never thought about the risks of being a pastor —especially being a bad pastor. That's when he started wondering whether he had what it took to do the job well. That reflection eventually led to doubts about himself because he couldn't figure out what made the difference.

Now for the first time in years he was beginning to understand some of the things that *could* make a difference. More importantly, he felt in that reflection a depth and substance he hadn't known before. He began to believe that he indeed did have the potential, and that God had finally opened the doors for him to begin to understand how to develop that potential.

He sprang to his feet and dashed back across the meadow and up the trail toward Inspiration Point. He jumped to touch a tree branch, hurled a few pine cones, and even chattered back at a woodpecker as he bounded up the trail. Before long he reached Inspiration Point and scrambled along the rocky crest to a rock outcropping that thrust like a bowsprit over the valley below. He perched on the end of the rock with his feet dangling over the edge.

The panoramic view stretched across the adjoining mountain ranges for at least fifty miles. The verdant green valley below was dotted with a few old farmhouses, an occasional herd of cows, and a small flock of sheep at the far end.

Frank prayed. First he offered thanks for the opportunity he had been given, then for the friendship of Kate and Charles and for the guidance they had given him. He gave thanks that he had been afforded the opportunity to look beyond the boundaries of his seminary training for the knowledge and insights he would need to be a good pastor. He thanked God for everything he could think of. For the confidence he was now feeling about his budding leadership skills. For the wonderful world we live in.

Then Frank prayed for God's continued guidance and the strength and courage to carry out his calling in a way that would bring glory and honor to God.

He had been praying for about an hour when he heard the brush crackling behind him. Charles appeared, sporting a backpack and a pair of binoculars.

"Mighty peaceful up here, isn't it?" Charles said.

"Divinely so," Frank replied.

"How was the hike up?"

"Inspirational, to say the least. No pun intended."

"I brought us a couple of sandwiches," Charles said as he opened his backpack, took out the sandwiches and two bottles of water.

"Thanks," Frank said. They both bowed their heads while Frank said grace, then quickly removed the wrappers from the sandwiches and began eating.

"Well, where did we leave off?" Charles asked.

"I'm not sure, but I know where I'd like to pick up," said Frank between bites.

"Where's that?"

"Let's say I do have the potential and I want to start leading myself in the right direction. Where do I start? I mean, what should I do first?"

Charles smiled. "Great question. The answer to leading self is the same as the answer for leading in any of the five contexts. It's a two-part answer. First you envision and then you initiate."

"Envision and initiate."

"That's it," Charles said. "Let's start with envisioning. In the self context it means for you to decide what kind of pastor you want to become."

"That's easy. A good one. And holy."

"That's a start. But you'll need a lot more specificity than that. What does 'good' mean to you? What will it mean to your parishioners? What does a *good job* look like to them? How will you know you're doing the job well? What does a good job look like to you? And to the bishop?"

"I've never really thought of it in those terms."

Charles reached into the backpack again for two bright red apples, a small stenographer's pad, and a pencil. He handed both to Frank.

"Time for some more note taking?" Frank asked.

"Nope. Time for some deep soul-searching and an assignment I'm going to let you complete by yourself."

"OK."

"I'm going to leave you up here by yourself again, so take as much time as you need to do the following. First complete the following sentence. *I am a pastor who ...* "

Frank wrote the sentence fragment across the top line of the first page of the notebook.

I am a pastor who ...

"Next, make a list in response to the following statement. *I make the following differences in the lives of my parishioners:*

Frank flipped the page and wrote across the top of the next page:

I make the following differences in the lives of my parishioners:

"Good," Charles said. "Now on the next page write, *I make the following differences in St. Joseph's Parish:*"

Frank flipped to the next page and wrote:

I make the following differences in St. Joseph's Parish:

A look of consternation came over his face. "But what if I can't get all the answers?"

"You won't get all the answers," Charles said as he stood and picked up his apple and the backpack. "But at least you'll get a start, which will begin to give you some perspective and direction. Take your time and we'll see you back at the cabin when you get there. Then we can talk about what you've come up with. There's no hurry. It's a beauty of a day, so enjoy it."

Charles got up, turned, and disappeared down the trail.

Frank reflected on their conversation, then turned to his assigned task. But each time he started to write something in the notebook, he stopped himself before the pencil hit the paper. He thought, *Is it right for me to decide what kind of pastor I should be? Or is that God's decision? Should I be steering the parish in a particular direction or should I just pray and let God's will be done? If I make a difference in the lives of my parishioners, am I doing God's will...or interfering with it?*

After a while he stood up, placed a rock on top of the pad so it wouldn't blow away, and walked around to the other side of the ridgeline. He hadn't added a single word to the pad since Charles' departure.

Finally he returned to the outcropping, took his seat overlooking the expansive valley below, and picked up the pad and pencil. He began tentatively, but soon became immersed in his writing until he completed the following list after "I am a pastor who:"

* Sanctifies, educates, and governs
* Touches my parishioners' lives in a way that brings them closer to God
* Touches my parishioners' lives in a way that brings them closer to one another
* Is a model of servant leadership
* Inspires people to join our parish
* Inspires people to attend Sunday Mass regularly
* Inspires people to attend daily Mass
* Helps people appreciate the Eucharist

- Helps people recognize God at work in the world around them
- Is respected and supported by staff
- Brings out the full potential of volunteers and lay staff
- Has the respect of other pastors
- Is seen by people as a positive example
- Is respected in the community
- Is worthy of my calling
- Is worthy in the eyes of God
- Is happy being a pastor
- Looks forward to each day

When he felt as though he might start repeating himself, Frank turned to the next page on the pad, which had, *"I make the following differences in the lives of my parishioners,"* written across the top. He again made a bulleted list:

- Help bring them closer to God
- Help them understand and appreciate their faith
- Show them how their faith can make a strong and positive difference in the world
- Help them to become instruments of God's peace and love
- Help them embrace the teachings of the Church
- Bring them closer to the Eucharist and all the Sacraments, especially Reconciliation
- Help them achieve their calling and full potential

He was reluctant to give up on this list even though it was shorter than the first one, but he finally decided to turn to the third page. It was even harder than the second. He finally managed to generate the following in response to the statement, *I make the following differences in St. Joseph's Parish:*

* Help create a spiritually healthy environment that is centered on the Sacraments
* See that parishioners have opportunities to learn more about the teachings of Jesus in ways that cause their faith to be nurtured and grow
* Cause the parish to grow both in numbers of parishioners and their involvement in parish life
* Make sure the parish serves those in need in our surrounding community

Frank noticed the sun dropping fast toward the line of mountain peaks to the west. Even though it didn't seem like it had taken much time to compile the lists—and they only comprised a few pages of listed items—he suddenly realized it had taken most of the afternoon to complete his assignment. He gathered his water bottle, pad, and pencil, and took off down the trail so he could reach the cabin before the rapidly falling sun disappeared behind the distant mountaintops.

He reached the cabin just as the shadows began to encroach upon the valley and the turkey vultures were settling *en masse* in the aspen grove. Kate and Charles sat on the deck outside the kitchen as he approached.

"I was just about to roll out one of the ATVs and come looking for you," Charles laughed.

"I'm not sure what happened to the afternoon," Frank said. "I was so intent on answering those questions you gave me that I lost track of the time."

"How about a snack?" Kate asked.

"Sounds great. These mountains always seem to make me hungry." He quickly bounded up the steps and joined Charles, as Kate ducked inside for some food.

"How'd it go?" his host asked.

"I don't know. I've got three lists, or maybe I should say one list, one part of a list, then a smaller part of a third one."

"Let's see."

Frank handed over the pad. "I don't know how good they are."

Kate returned with water for everyone and a tray full of hors d'ouvres. Frank downed half his water and dove into the goodies as Charles perused the list.

"This is great," he said.

"Really?" Frank shrugged. "It seems somewhat chaotic and sloppy to me."

"This is your first take on these. Of course you'll want to refine them, get the lists pared down to a few manageable statements, and so on. But for a first effort, this is pretty darn good."

"You're not just saying that, are you?"

"That wouldn't serve you well, would it?" Charles said. "I can only help you by being truly honest. These lists are a great start."

"It was harder than I thought it would be," said Frank as he downed another hors d'ouvre.

"Sounds like it made you think."

"It made me think differently than the way I've been thinking. It took me a while to come at it from a different perspective. Thinking of myself in that role wasn't all that easy at first, but when I finally stopped focusing on all my inadequacies it became less stressful. Not easier, necessarily, but a lot less stressful. Then I realized that I hadn't given an ounce of thought to those last two questions and they're probably the most important ones I should be focusing on right now."

"All three are important," Charles said.

"How do you think Monsignor Firko would have answered them?" Frank asked.

"I don't know. But it's a great question, because I'm sure he couldn't have been as good a pastor as he was without answering them on some level."

"I can see that."

"But if you think his answers are going to be the right answers for you, you'd better think again."

"But he did a good job," Frank protested.

Charles shook his head. "A good job for *him* as pastor. A good job for *you* as pastor may be different. I'm not saying you shouldn't learn from his success. Of course you should. You should learn from everyone you can, just like you're learning from me today. But don't compare yourself to him in a judgmental way. And, most importantly, don't try to be someone you're not. Your gifts are unique to you just as his were unique to him. Learn from Monsignor Firko how to bring out the best in yourself."

"Sounds to me like you got off to a great start getting in touch with yourself today," Kate said.

Frank nodded. "I hope so. Where do I go from here?"

"Over the next week or so, review and re-review what you've written," Charles said. "Feel free to add to the list, edit it, or delete items that seem redundant or not important. Pray about it. Talk to Father Manion to get his insights about what he's observed at St. Joseph's while he's been there. Ask him what he sees as the parish's strengths and weaknesses. Find out what he likes most about it and what he dislikes. Ask him what he would change if he were made pastor. Talk to a few mainstream parishioners and ask the same questions. Compare all their answers to your lists, modifying them appropriately. Continue the process until you have confidence that if you could achieve the outcomes you've listed, then St. Joe's would be on track and you'd feel good about your work there."

"That's it, then?" Frank asked.

"Well, that's the beginning," Charles said as Kate smiled. "The beginning of the first step, which you'll recall I referred to as 'envisioning.'"

"So these lists will be my vision for myself in the role of pastor," Frank said, although it was as much a question as it was a statement.

"Let's call it the first draft or first generation of your vision. You'll refine it as you continue to learn firsthand about the parish and its people. But this draft will do for now to give you a direction and a focus as you transition into the new role."

"That makes sense. But mentioning 'envisioning' reminded me that you said there was another step— 'initiating' if I remember correctly. When does that come?"

Charles smiled. "You've got a great memory. We'll talk about initiating tomorrow morning before you head back. I don't want to put your mind on overload so you can't reflect on these lists. Let's eat some dinner then we'll watch a movie or something."

The dinner conversation was lively as Frank quizzed both Kate and Charles on their assessments about the strengths or shortcomings of different pastors they had observed during the past several decades. It was intriguing to him that in almost every case the priests in question were devout and holy men. The variability in outcomes they experienced in their parishes resulted from their varying levels of ability in dealing with people, problem solving, managing conflict, making viable decisions, and organizational skills. What it finally came down to was the inescapable conclusion that faith and spirituality were essential foundations—there could never be any doubt about that—and that building a community of faith grounded in Catholic doctrine and theology was the essential outcome. But the new insight for Frank was that leadership practices primarily determined how well a pastor could build a community of faith from his *own* spiritual foundation. Those pastors who developed what he was now beginning to call 'leadership competencies' produced magnificent outcomes. Those who didn't paid the price in diminished results.

This revelation was huge for Frank because it was something he'd never considered before. But equally significant for him was that he was now on a path toward learning what he needed to know to be a good pastor. For the first time he was excited about this opportunity God was offering. He was being called to serve Him and the people of St. Joseph's in a very special way.

Later that night after Evening Prayer, Frank went to his room, laid his breviary on the night stand next to his bed, and took out his Bible.

He turned to the Book of Jeremiah and carefully read chapter one, verses four through ten, while reflecting on all that had happened during the day. Jeremiah's call to become a prophet to the nations came early in life, just as Father Frank's calling to the priesthood had come at a young age. Jeremiah's calling terrified him in many ways. Jeremiah must have felt the same inadequacies that he had experienced, Frank pondered.

The most important parallel, however, was that both Jeremiah and Frank failed to see that God's call and empowerment always match. When God calls on us to do something, He always equips us to fulfill that calling.

This realization was the one that provided the most comfort to Frank. Before, when he was scared about the task ahead, his greatest concern was that he didn't see the opportunity as one where he would grow. Because he didn't see that avenue, he subconsciously feared that maybe being a pastor wasn't his true calling. *God always provides the empowerment to fulfill His true callings.* Fortunately, the Forrests provided that avenue. And even though his personal development would likely continue for the rest of his life, at least he could feel peace that he was on the right path. He experienced a great sense of relief that he had responded to Kate's offer of help and listened to the wisdom she and Charles had to offer.

He couldn't help but think about the story of the man whose house was threatened by a flood. A policeman came by and suggested he evacuate because the floodwaters were rising and were a threat to him and his house. The man replied that he didn't need to because he had faith that God would save him. He would stay and pray. The floodwaters reached the man's house and flooded the entire first floor, forcing the man to the second story. He leaned out the window as a man in a boat came by and offered to evacuate him before the flood worsened. The man again responded that he didn't need to because he had faith that God would save him. He would stay and pray. The floodwaters rose even more, forcing the man to his roof. A helicopter flew overhead and offered to lift the man to safety. Again he replied he had faith and would pray. The floodwaters soon swept the house and the man away, and the man drowned. The man showed up at the gates of heaven greatly confused. Upon meeting God, the man asked Him why He hadn't answered his prayers. God replied, "I sent you a policeman, a boat, and a helicopter. I don't know what else I could have done!"

Frank smiled as he rolled over in bed, confident that he had answered God's calling and that God had answered his prayers.

Frank awoke at the crack of dawn on Saturday morning feeling more rested, refreshed, and invigorated than he had felt in a long time. He quietly slipped outside into the brisk morning air and made his way to a hillside trail, where the Forrests had installed the Stations of the Cross. He took about 45 minutes to meditate on the Stations, then returned to the house to celebrate Mass with Kate and Charles before breakfast.

After breakfast the three took off on a hike toward Fish Creek. The vultures were migrating out of the aspen grove and into the morning sunlight to warm their feathers.

"Can we talk about initiating now?" Frank asked.

"Yes, but first a bit more about contexts before we leave envisioning," Charles said. "What context have we been operating in until now?"

"Self, or leading self."

"Right. We've been creating your personal vision, so we've been carrying out the envisioning function in the self-context."

"Got it."

"As a leader, what would you see yourself doing at the envisioning stage if you were in the one-to-one context?"

Frank thought for a moment. "Would I be helping someone else create a vision for his or her role?"

"You got it," Charles said. "You see, everyone has to be a self-leader to some extent. One of your first responsibilities in leading others is to help them lead themselves. So as we learn about envisioning and initiating in the self context, I also want you to think about it in the one-to-one context, because much of what you'll be doing is facilitating these processes with other people."

"What about the other three contexts?"

"You'll have to come back in a few weeks to get into more detail about them. I think it best that you start by understanding and applying the envisioning process for yourself first and then try using it with others. We'll expand to the other contexts after you've had a chance to work on the first two."

"Fair enough," Frank said. "But what I hear you saying is that one of the first things I should do when I take over at St. Joseph's is to talk with the key staff members there and make sure they have a clear vision about their own roles and how they see that impacting the parishioners and the parish."

Charles nodded. "Bingo … No pun intended. With that you've also taken your first step toward initiating."

"I have? How?"

"Initiating involves creating a list–or sometimes we call it an agenda–of goals and action items that will lead to the accomplishment of your vision. Since you've said that one of the things you're going to want to do at St. Joseph's–no matter how you end up wording it–is to bring out the best in your staff, or help them perform to their fullest potential in their various roles. Then, a great starting point is to also have each person create his or her own vision. Just like you have started to do."

"Good," Frank said, reflecting on all this. He also began to realize how helpful it would have been had he gone through this with Monsignor Meeker in his last job. The only nagging concerns he'd had about working with the man had been the occasions when he seemed to be moving in one direction while sensing that the Monsignor thought he should be doing something different. It never occurred to him to approach the pastor and ask him about it. Frank had always dismissed the concerns by concluding that if the pastor had felt there was a problem, he would have said something.

"So you've just taken your first step toward initiating," Charles said.

"How so?"

"Part of your vision is to bring out the best in your staff. Therefore, an initiative that would help you achieve this is to have each of them work on drafting a personal vision statement that you can review, discuss with him or her, and revise as necessary."

"So, in essence, initiating is the process for turning vision into action."

"You got it. Once the vision is clear, the next step is to create a list of goals and action items that will lead toward the accomplishment of the vision."

"What else should go on my list?" Frank asked.

"Let's not forget it's *your* list," Charles replied. "But we've discussed a couple of other items that make sense to me. For example, one was to talk to Father Manion about his assessment of things at St. Joseph's and to get his suggestions about what your priorities ought to be."

"Right. And then talk to some of the parishioners as well. I'll bet some of the people at the diocese have opinions also."

"Good thinking."

"What else?"

"Think about all the things you listed yesterday while you were writing the foundation for your personal vision. Focus on those that are most important to you now. Then think of some meaningful action you can take that will help breathe life into those priorities."

Frank thought for a moment. "One issue that kept repeating itself in my thinking yesterday was being able to bring people closer to the Eucharist. An obvious way to do that would be to increase attendance at daily Mass."

"How many people attend daily Mass at St. Joseph's now?"

"I don't know."

"What kind of priority was that for Monsignor Firko? What time is daily Mass? Who mostly attends?"

"I don't know those answers either."

"That's OK," Charles said. "The point here is that in the beginning most of your activity should consist of research. You should spend a lot of time asking questions of the right people and then listening. You'll want to ask questions about the type of results people are producing and how those results tie into your initial vision. You'll also want to find out in what ways they think they've been supported or not supported in the past. Also ask what they think are their greatest future challenges. Your investigation will confirm some of your ideas, cause you to modify others, and will undoubtedly lead you to completely abandon others. Throughout the process you'll reshape your initial vision and refine it until it makes total sense.

And hopefully you'll be leading your key staff members through the same process along with you."

"So rather than me having all the answers when I come through the door, it's more about knowing what questions to ask."

"I believe you're going to be a great pastor," Kate said, as they reached the top of the canyon overlooking Fish Creek.

"Well, with your help, I think I can at least avoid being a really bad one," Frank laughed. "I don't know how I'll ever be able to thank you."

"Our thanks will come when you prove to be the really good one we know you have the potential to become," Kate said.

They explored the banks of Fish Creek for a while, taking note of some beautiful columbine flowers that had just started to bloom. They made it back to the cabin and completed Midday Prayer before having an early lunch so Father Frank could get back to help Monsignor Meeker with the Saturday evening and Sunday Masses at St. Mary's.

Lost in thought, Frank turned onto the highway for the journey back to St. Mary's. His mind was filled with ideas, his heart filled with enthusiasm as he looked forward to finding out more details about the situation at St. Joseph's and the opportunities and challenges that awaited him.

About halfway home, an image came to mind about how to organize what he'd learned so far. He pulled over at one of the scenic overlooks, took the notepad he'd been using to capture his ideas over the last few days, and created the following sketch:

At the center of everything is my spiritual foundation or core spiritual self, he thought. *The next level of progression outward is the rest of my personality. My spiritual foundation and personality then form the basis for everything I do as a leader in each of five contexts, which include: leading self, leading others in one-to-one relationships, leading teams and groups, leading organizations, and leading alliances.* He still wasn't too clear on alliances, so he put a question mark next to it, reminding himself that he would delve into it more deeply in future conversations with Charles. *I still haven't shown that envisioning and initiating are the two beginning activities in each of the five contexts,* he thought. *But that's OK. I'll just remember them for now and figure out a way to add them to my diagram later.*

Pleased with his effort and thinking that these previously foreign concepts were starting to gain clarity in his mind, Frank closed the notepad and pulled back onto the freeway to complete his journey home.

❦

The following Monday he eagerly phoned Father James Manion.

"I was beginning to wonder when I'd hear from you," Father Manion said after the two exchanged pleasantries.

Frank laughed. "Let's just say I was in the throes of pastoral formation. I'm eager to get together and find out what you've seen and to hear any suggestions you might have."

"Great. Let's meet for lunch and we'll go from there."

"How about Gus' Place?"

"Works for me. See you at noon."

Gus' had the best cold lunch platter known to humankind. It consisted of salami, provolone cheese and capricola ham that was extra lean with just the right amount of spices, along with a basket of bread and some semi-mild green peppers. The sliced French bread was cooked East Coast style with a flaky exterior crust and a light, fluffy interior. If you piled on just the right amount of cheese, salami, and capricola, you thought you were eating a sandwich straight from heaven. When you followed that with a bite from one of Gus' special peppers…well, it was easy to see why Gus' was a favorite lunch place.

"Monsignor Meeker's planning on me helping with the daily Masses for the rest of this week, then I'm pretty much finished with any duties there," Frank said. "How about if I spend the rest of my time this week with you at St. Joe's finding my way around, then we split the weekend Masses and I'll take over from there."

James nodded. "That would work for me. You're going to like this parish a lot."

"I'm beginning to think I will."

"Like every parish, it has its good points and the not so good, but all in all it should turn out to be a fine assignment. If I weren't going to Rome, I'd jump at the chance to be assigned here as pastor."

"What are some of the not-so-good things you've seen?" Frank asked.

"You'll see them, too, soon enough," James shrugged. "One of the more interesting ones is the music director. When I first encountered her, I couldn't figure out what on earth Monsignor Firko had been thinking. She's been here longer than the Rocky Mountains—or at least as long. I guess he didn't have the heart or the courage to replace her."

"What's the problem?"

"I think she learned about Catholic music and developed her attitudes about song while sucking on lemons. It seems she thinks that in order to become holy, people have to suffer through Mass and she's willing to provide that suffering through really bad performances."

Frank smiled. It wasn't the first story he'd ever heard about dour music directors, but he'd never considered the possibility that he'd have to confront one. Maybe he'd just duck this issue.

"You get that one turned around and the parishioners of St. Joseph's will honor you forever," James said.

They spent the next couple of hours enjoying their lunch and sharing information about the lay of the land at St. Joseph's.

"There's one final thought I'd like to leave with you," James said.

"I'm all ears."

"It's something my grandfather said years ago; it's one of my father's favorite stories about him. My grandfather was suffering from an extended illness and a friend asked him how he was coping with it. His response was, 'I know God won't give me a cross bigger than I can bear. But if He does, I know He'll send along a Simon to help me carry it.'"

"That's powerful."

"Let me be one of your Simons," James said.

As Frank drove back to the rectory at St. Mary's, the thought occurred to him how much greener the grass always looked on the other side of the fence. He could name a number of parishes that had excellent reputations, but when he'd gotten an insider's look, either as a deacon or as an assistant, they all had their issues. Their strengths were real, of course, but so were their imperfections. It reminded him of a conversation he overheard in his childhood. His father invited a few friends from the parish to the house to play cards. During the game a couple of them started criticizing the local diocese. After listening for a short time, his father cut them off by saying, "Stop griping about your Church. If it were perfect, you couldn't belong."

Frank finally concluded that if he were going to be an effective pastor, he needed to learn how to deal with imperfection using timely and practical approaches.

He decided to amend his personal vision to state that he would be a pastor who would deal with issues and solve problems when they arise, rather than let them linger while praying for them to go away. This, in turn, led him to the uncomfortable realization that he would have to deal with Mrs. Mediocre Music Director.

The rest of the week passed quickly. Frank spent a lot of time with Father James, learning how everything worked at St. Joseph's. He met a few parishioners and all the staff, but didn't spend much time with them because he wanted to maximize the limited number of days available with his energetic priest friend.

The weekend Masses went smoothly. The parishioners at Father Frank's Masses all applauded politely when he introduced himself. Most of them extended personal welcomes afterward. But he also discovered firsthand why James had raised the issue of the music director. Frank hadn't heard music that bad in years. *James was right*, he thought. *She probably was sucking on lemons when she learned about music.* He renewed his commitment to address the problem.

On Monday he thanked Father James and bade him farewell. It gave him comfort to know that James would be nearby for a couple more months should he need to call on him for help, even though he didn't know what kind of need might arise.

Then Father Frank settled in to the tasks associated with assuming his pastoral role.

His meeting with the office manager went smoothly. Annette was courteous, organized, and likeable. It was clear from the outset she wanted the transition to go smoothly and that her top priority was to make Father Frank's tenure as pleasant as possible. They were going to get along just fine. He also had a sense she was plugged into the parish grapevine so he could get a lot of useful information from her about what parishioners were thinking, although she clearly wasn't a busybody or a gossip. He felt she'd be someone he could trust, which confirmed Father James's assessment as well.

Later in the day, Father Frank met with the director of religious education. M.J. also exuded an air of quiet competence and seemed to have a good handle on her job and its responsibilities. Like Annette, when he asked her to complete a visioning assignment similar to the one he had done with Charles, she was enthusiastic. The prospect of reviewing her direction and setting priorities with the new pastor pleased her.

Soon after, Annette said that she had spoken to Astrid, the music director, who had given her the third degree. "She wanted to know why you wanted to meet with her, what the problem was, and what she should do to prepare. She also asked how long the meeting would take, who else would be there, and who else you had met with before her. She said she was really busy and didn't know if she could work it into her schedule this week."

"This week?" Frank asked. "I wanted to meet with her today if possible, and if not, then tomorrow. Did you answer her questions?"

"I just said I didn't know. I told her you were meeting with everyone individually and that most people were looking forward to it. She said she'd try to stop by later this afternoon."

"We'll see what happens," Frank said as the youth minister entered. They went into Frank's office and had a meeting similar to the others. It put him at ease to see that people enjoyed talking about their roles and their vision for those roles, and that they were excited that Frank took a personal interest in what they were doing.

At 4:30 in the afternoon, just as Annette was getting ready to leave for the day, Astrid walked stiffly into the office.

"Oh, hi, Astrid," Annette said.

"Good afternoon," Astrid replied coldly as she strode past Annette with barely a glance and disappeared into Father Frank's office, closing the door firmly behind her.

Father Frank looked up. "Good afternoon, Astrid."

"If you want a different approach to the music offerings here at St. Joseph's, then you'll have to talk to someone else," she declared.

"What do you mean?" Father Frank asked, somewhat taken aback.

"I think you know. Your first day here and your most important priority is to call me on the carpet. You haven't even seen all the Masses yet."

"I'm not calling anyone on the carpet …"

"All you youngsters who've come up since Vatican II want to change everything without even knowing what it is you're changing."

Frank thought, *Vatican II?*

Before he could respond, she continued, "It doesn't matter to me anymore, as I've decided it's time to retire. So I'm here to tender my resignation, effective as soon as you find someone to replace me. I've put in 30 years with almost no gratitude, but for the thankfulness of our Lord. It's time for someone else to fight all these battles."

"Are you sure?" asked Frank. Realizing the magnitude of what she'd said he quickly determined he didn't want to talk her out of it. But he also didn't want to get his hopes up and have her change her mind later.

"I've been thinking about it for quite some time. Monsignor Firko, God rest his soul, and I had some discussions about it before he passed on, but I just didn't see how I could leave him high and dry. It wouldn't have been fair. But now you're here, you're young, and you've got your own ideas, so it's time for me to move on."

"Well, thanks for giving me time to find someone else; that's very thoughtful of you. I'll work quickly to find a replacement, although I don't think we can really replace 30 years. But we'll try to find someone who'll work hard to follow in your footsteps."

"I guess that's it, then," she stated. "I'll see you on Sunday." She turned and left. The meeting hadn't lasted more than three minutes.

"That was short," Annette said as Father Frank emerged from his office.

"She quit," he said.

"Quit?"

"Well, retired. She gave notice. She's leaving."

"Hallelujah! Hallelujah!" Annette sang quietly as Frank frowned. "Oh, I'm sorry. I don't want to sound mean or anything, but this is good news. Good news for you, good news for me, and good news for the parish. People will think you're a miracle worker."

Frank shrugged. "I hope not. I'm still trying to figure out what happened."

"See you tomorrow," Annette said as she walked out the door.

Father Frank returned to his work not knowing whether he should be excited or disappointed. On the one hand, Astrid's sudden and unexpected departure was clearly good news. All he had to do to get a good music program going in the parish was to hire a competent music director to replace her. But on the other hand, he felt somewhat slighted. He felt cheated out of the opportunity to deal with the issue. He had spent a great deal of energy thinking about how to proceed with Astrid and open up the lines of communication, and then poof!—just like that, it was all over. It was like getting all psyched up to push against a stone wall and then reaching out to touch the barrier only to discover it was made of vapor.

Later that night after his Evening Prayer, the concern still lingered. Even though he had talked himself into accepting the fact that the resolution with Astrid was a good one, he still felt a twinge of emptiness. Had he done something wrong? Should he have said something different? He dozed off with all sorts of questions bouncing around like pinballs in his brain.

The next morning Frank awakened much refreshed, eagerly looking forward to his first meeting with the parish council. He had met a few members in passing at Mass on Sunday, but had not yet had the opportunity to get to know any of them.

Annette had kept most of the day open on his calendar so he could prepare for the meeting, which was scheduled for 7:00 p.m. Fortunately, she had prepared a proposed agenda. She used the same template that Monsignor Firko had always used. She'd also organized the back-up information he needed, such as financial reports, a report from the facilities sub-committee, and an outline of the presentation submitted by the Summer Festival committee chairwoman.

The first thing he realized was that he had no clue what the financial reports meant. He thought it meant there was money in the bank. But he didn't know if it was enough. *Who pays the bills?* he wondered. *For that matter, who makes the deposits? Who counts the collections? What are our expenses? Who is the bookkeeper? How much are our collections and how much are our expenses?* He felt overwhelmed again, so he called Annette into his office for help.

"Marion is the bookkeeper," she explained. "She does more than just keep the books, though. She oversees all the financial concerns of the parish. She's a C.P.A. and is really smart. Monsignor let her pretty much do everything and asked just to be kept informed. She said she'd be available before the parish council meeting if you wanted to go over things."

"Good. Can you schedule that? I think we'll need at least fifteen minutes."

"I'll allow more time than that just in case you need it—maybe an hour."

"And I need your help with a couple of other things," he said. "I can see that I'm going to need to rely on you a lot to tell me what people in the parish are saying about different things that happen."

"I did that for Monsignor," she replied.

"But I also need to know about the people themselves."

Annette looked at him curiously. "I'm not a gossip."

"I don't want to hear gossip," Frank explained. "But I don't know the history of the parish or the people. And when issues come up—like the one with Astrid—I'm going to need some help in understanding the background. So part of your role is to help keep me informed about issues that might be brewing in the parish."

"I'll do my best," Annette said. "But talking about other people makes me uncomfortable. Anyway, you'll probably have a lot of questions after the parish council meeting tonight."

*A*nnette *was right about needing more time to understand the finances*, Frank thought as he and Marion wrapped up their meeting to bring him up to speed on the parish's fiscal situation. The meeting had lasted an hour and fifteen minutes, and easily could have gone longer if they weren't already late for the parish council meeting.

The five parish council members stopped chatting and rose from the conference table to greet Father Frank and Marion as the two joined them in the library. Frank re-introduced himself to each of them, then took the only available seat, to the right of Mrs. Dobie. He thought it was an interesting coincidence that she reminded him of a Doberman pinscher as she sat up straight as a board at the head of the table, peering at the group over a thick stack of papers. He chased the thought from his mind. *Charity in all things*, he reasoned.

"Now that Father is finally here we can begin," she said. "Father, would you lead us in prayer, please?"

Frank asked God to bless and guide the group in their deliberations and to watch over the members as they fulfilled their roles for the betterment of the parish.

"Thank you, Father," Mrs. Dobie said. "Marion? Would you please review the finances?"

It hadn't occurred to Frank that someone else might chair the meeting. He wondered, *Did she have the same agenda as his?* He felt somewhat relieved that he wouldn't have to *ad lib* his way through his first parish council meeting. He was also slightly amused at Mrs. Dobie's officiousness. *This might turn out to be fun to watch*, he mused.

Marion handed out a short one-page summary of the parish's financial situation and briefly described the information on it.

"Thank you, Marion," Mrs. Dobie said. "Next on the agenda is old business."

"Can we ask questions about Marion's report?" Rob Demgen said.

"We have a full agenda this evening and not much time to waste. Is it a long question?"

"No, but don't you think we should discuss the fiscal situation of the parish when the financial report is presented?" Rob shot back.

"Well, not if it's going to interfere with the important business we have to conduct," the resolute Mrs. Dobie replied. "If it's going to be a long question it would be better to discuss it some other time, so we can get on with the meeting."

"The question isn't that long. But I don't know how long the answer will be until I hear it and I can't hear it until I ask the question."

"Maybe we'd better wait then. It sounds like we could get sidetracked and then we'll be here all night and not get the important things discussed."

"Aren't financial matters important?" Rob asked. "It's part of our responsibility to know the financial condition of the parish so we can exercise proper stewardship."

"Marion just gave us a summary of the financial condition of the parish." Mrs. Dobie would not give an inch. "And then she explained it so we could all understand it."

Rob nodded. "I was right here for the entire presentation. And now I have a simple question about what was presented."

"Financial questions are never simple. You should know that by now."

"All I want to know is whether our cash reserves have been increasing or decreasing during the first half of the year," Rob said as he turned toward Marion with a pleading look in his eyes.

"Except for a slight dip in the month of February, they've steadily increased each month this year," Marion answered. "That could be because February was a short month. It's really nothing to worry about."

"Thank you." Mrs. Dobie scowled. "Now if there are no further disruptions, it's time to discuss old business."

Marion winked at Rob, who replied by raising his eyebrows and shaking his head in disbelief. Everyone else took the encounter in stride, as Father Frank wondered what he had inherited. Annette's warning that he would have a lot of questions after the parish council meeting began to take on new meaning.

"The first item under old business is for the DVD player and TV that M.J. wants to get for the catechists to use in our religious education classes. Have we found anyone who has one they'd like to donate?"

"Do we all get copies of the agenda?" Jerry Blamey said. Jerry, a scholarly looking man in his late 50s, wore a thin pair of reading glasses far down on his nose. He peered over the top of them as he awaited Mrs. Dobie's answer.

"We decided not to bother making copies for everyone because it uses up too much paper," Mrs. Dobie replied.

"Who is 'we'?" Jerry asked. "I think I've been to all the meetings and I don't remember that decision."

"I have the agenda right here. I assure you everything will be covered, *if* people will provide me with an opportunity to follow it."

"Well, is Father's installation Mass and celebration with the Bishop on your agenda?" Jerry asked.

"Because the Knights of Columbus have some ideas about the dinner that could make it really great."

It occurred to Frank that the agenda Annette had given him was, indeed, different than Mrs. Dobie's, but he decided not to make it an issue at this point.

"It's under new business because we haven't discussed it before," Mrs. Dobie replied. "New business follows old business on the agenda."

"How much stuff do you have under old business?" Jerry asked. "Because we don't have much time to plan and organize the installation dinner and the Knights want to know what freedom we have to move forward."

"Before we do that," M.J. interjected, "could we please get approval for me to buy the DVD player and TV for my catechists?"

Father Frank listened, stunned. Not one of them had acknowledged his presence in the room after the greetings. *How did Monsignor Firko ever get anything done?* he thought. *Even more important, how will I ever get anything done?* He sat back as a detached but interested observer for the remainder of the meeting as they bantered back and forth, bouncing from topic to topic, never reaching a conclusion about anything, and arguing over the most insignificant issues. The topic of his installation was broached at least a dozen times in the overall discussion, but never once was his opinion sought. *At least they're consistent*, he thought. *They haven't asked me about anything. Nor, for that matter, have they even given me an opportunity to get a word in edgewise.*

By the end of the meeting, Frank had a headache and felt claustrophobic. All he wanted to do was escape. He quickly slipped away to the solace of the rectory and his breviary for Evening Prayer.

By the time he was ready for bed his headache had lessened. He tossed and turned fitfully until well past midnight, then finally dozed off. But the images of the parish council meeting kept replaying over and over in his head. It reminded him of the time he and his best friend in high school had first learned chess and played all day long. That night, no matter how hard he tried he couldn't get the images of chess pieces and the chessboard out of his thoughts. This was much worse, however, because instead of inanimate objects, these were images of real people sniping back and forth at one another. And they were all people he would have to deal with tomorrow. And the next day. And next week. And next month. And next year. *They aren't going away and neither am I,* he mused, as feelings of claustrophobia threatened to envelop him again.

It was sometime around 1 a.m. that the Lord finally threw Frank a life raft. It hit him like a bolt of lightning. *I should call Kate and Charles Forrest.* The very thought caused him to sit upright in the morning darkness. *Why didn't I think of that sooner?* Realizing that a call at this hour would be socially unacceptable, Frank lay back down, rolled over, thanked the Lord, and dozed off peacefully for a few hours before rising for morning Mass.

After Mass he hurried to his office to phone the Forrests.

"I need help!" he almost yelled into the phone when Kate answered.

"What's wrong? Are you okay?"

"Much is wrong. The music director quit and my parish council looks and acts worse than Congress in an election year. I'm at a complete loss. Talk about a fish out of water. I'm a whale out of the entire ocean."

"Can you come up to the ranch this week? We're planning on being there anyway, and it would be a good place to work it all through. See if Father Manion can cover your daily Masses through the end of the week and then you can stay until Saturday again."

"I'm sure he will. He already offered to and he enjoys celebrating daily Mass at St. Joseph's. But I don't know if three days will be enough time. We're talking about a major salvage job here."

"It's not as bad as you think," Kate said. "But if we need more time, I'm sure Charles will have a reasonable suggestion."

Frank couldn't help but notice how soothed he felt as a result of the conversation. *Why do I always feel so much better after talking to them?* he wondered.

He immediately called Father James, who said he'd be glad to cover Frank's Masses for the remainder of the week. Father James and Annette agreed to tell people that Father Frank had been called away unexpectedly on personal business and would return on Saturday.

Nearing the cabin, Frank drove with a great sense of urgency, barely noticing the turkey vultures as he passed the aspen grove.

Kate and Charles met him at the front entrance and they immediately settled into the massive sofas in the living room as Frank began to unburden himself of his worries. He wanted them to know the entire picture, so he started by explaining how he had taken Annette, M.J., and the others through their envisioning and initiating exercises.

"And they liked it?" Kate asked.

"They really did. They seemed pleased that I had taken a personal interest in them and what they were doing. And they also seemed to enjoy the opportunity to talk about what they want to do in the future."

"Sounds like there's no problem so far," Kate said.

"Then came Astrid …" Frank recounted his encounter with the mediocre music director.

"And that experience left you feeling bad," Charles said.

"Yeah, but I'm not sure why."

"Probably because she made you feel guilty. Like her leaving was your fault."

Frank shrugged. "That's some of it I guess. But it also feels like she still has a lot of anger directed toward me and it's just sort of out there."

"So even though she's departed, there's no closure."

"Yeah, I think that's probably the biggest issue."

"That's easy enough," Charles said. "The next time there's a major parish social function, recognize her publicly for her service to the parish all these years. Get her a nice gift–Annette can probably tell you what she'd like–and thank her in front of everyone."

"What if everyone thinks she owes them an apology for what she subjected them to all those years?"

Charles laughed as he wagged a finger. "Ah, ah, ah. We'll have none of that."

"Sorry," Frank said. "You had to be there to fully appreciate that comment. What happens if she won't attend?"

"Find out from Annette if she was close to anyone. Bring the friend into the plan. Maybe even let the friend pick out the present. Then make it the friend's responsibility to get Astrid to the event."

Great idea. I can do that, Frank thought to himself, *No wonder Charles is a super success. He can probably make anything happen if it involves people.*

"Was that your big concern?" Charles asked.

"One of them. But it pales in comparison to the next one."

"Which is?"

"The parish council."

"Tell us about it," Kate urged.

They listened intently as he described the chaotic meeting and the bizarre behavior of the majority of the council members. He ended by saying, "I don't see any way that sitting down with each of them individually is going to change much. I'm afraid they'll just get back together and it'll be like pushing the reset button. The craziness will just start up again."

Charles nodded. "You're probably right."

"What should I do?" Frank asked. "I don't think I can just fire them all and start with an all new council. I don't even think I can replace one or two of them without setting off all kinds of fireworks."

"You're probably right about that, too," Charles said. "I don't think firing one or more of them is the place to start. However, when you eventually do replace some of them, which is inevitable, remember to do so with care."

"You think they're salvageable?"

"I believe you should be thinking about salvaging the council as an entity and not be so focused on the individual members. This is where we start talking about leading in the team context."

"I remember that," Frank said as he pulled out the notebook he had used during his last visit. He turned it to the page where he had sketched his rendition of the contextual leadership model Charles had outlined during their previous meeting.

"What do you think of this?" He showed it to Charles and Kate.

Kate nodded. "Very creative."

"I agree. Now let me show you something else." Charles reached over and took the notebook from Frank. "Taken together, all five contexts form the acronym SOTOA. If you want to get fancy, the way we do in the corporate world, you can call it the SOTOA model for contextual leadership."

Charles then proceeded to write the following below Frank's diagram in the notebook:

Leading Self	= S
Leading Others One-to-One	= O
Leading Teams	= T
Leading Organizations	= O
Leading Alliances	= A

He handed the notebook back to Frank. "There you have it."

Frank studied it for a moment. "Do you know that the Greek word for 'savior' is *soter*?"

"I've never heard that before," Charles answered.

"How would it be if for my own use I change the word 'alliances' to 'relationships'? I'd of course be referring to the more significant and meaningful relationships the parish might foster."

"I don't see anything wrong with that," Charles said.

"It'll help to remind me that our Savior will always be our ultimate leadership model, but it's useful to think in practical terms, depending on the context in which I'm leading."

"That's really creative." Kate was genuinely impressed.

"From here on out I'll remember this framework as SOTOR, or the SOTOR model of contextual leadership, because it sounds like *soter*."

"Great," Kate and Charles said in unison.

"Later on it occurred to me that I could add concentric circles outside the core ring to show how envisioning and initiating fall into each context."

"Wow," Charles exclaimed. "Why don't you go ahead and add those rings here and let's see what it looks like?"

"OK." Frank proceeded to add two more rings. "How's this?"

SOTOR Model for Pastoral Leadership

Leading Self

Envisioning

Leading Others One-to-One

Leading Key Relationships

Core Spiritual Self

Personality

Initiating

Leading Organizations

Leading Teams

"I really like that," Charles said. "I like the way it shows that your personality and spiritual self interacts with all five contexts. But I especially like the way it shows that even though you'll have separate visions and initiatives in each context, they're all interconnected."

"I find this helpful in understanding how everything ties together," Frank said. "It helps me to simplify something that otherwise might be overwhelming."

"You're really getting this. Now let's learn about teams."

"Do you think I should view my parish council as a team?" Frank tried to figure out how to relate those two disparate images in his mind. Team and parish council—this was way beyond being an oxymoron. He struggled to find a noun that fit better than team. *Maybe a word like crowd, mob, gang, or gaggle,* he thought. *What do you call a group of kangaroos? Or clowns?*

"You're having trouble seeing them as a team because no one ever taught them how to act as a team—to demonstrate true teamwork," Charles said.

Frank shrugged. "That's stating the obvious." He thought, *Maybe they learned their skills at a pie-throwing contest.*

"So as the pastor and leader of the parish, you'll have to be the one to teach them."

"I was afraid that's where this was heading," Frank said. "They don't even *listen* to each other, let alone cooperate. To think of them working as a team is like trying to imagine a half-dozen pit bulls in a ring trying to teach other how to stand on their hind legs, and performing the can-can in unison."

"It won't be that hard—if you do it right."

"It's doing it right that's the hard part."

"That's why we're here, isn't it?" said Charles as Frank reluctantly nodded his agreement. "Well then, where do you think we should start?"

"With envisioning?"

"You got it."

"We never talked about how to do envisioning with a group or team."

"I know," Charles said. "And we didn't talk about doing it with the organization, either. So during this visit I'll show you how to do both so you can start bringing order to some of the chaos when you get back."

"I'm all ears." Frank flipped to the next blank page in his notebook.

"Envisioning is carried out by whoever creates the team. It involves defining the scope and boundaries of focus for team activities, delineating team membership requirements and basic structure, spelling out who the team reports to and what the team's basic responsibilities involve. As for your parish council, much of this will be spelled out in directives from the diocese, but there will be other elements you'll have to determine for yourself."

"I've seen some of those directives."

"Once you've developed the vision for the team—in this case your parish council—then you can complete the initiating process. This involves creating a team charter. A team charter consists of five components, which include: a clear definition of purpose; a statement of anticipated outcomes; operating guidelines; a list of team norms; and clearly delineated roles and responsibilities for each of the members."

Frank numbered and listed the five components in his notebook:

Team Charter:
1. Clear definition of team purpose
2. A statement of anticipated outcomes
3. Operating guidelines
4. A list of team norms to guide individual behavior
5. Clearly delineated team roles and responsibilities for each member

He showed the list to Charles. "How's that?"

"Perfect. The key is to create the charter before you actually do any teamwork, so you can use the guidelines to guide your efforts. Many of the problems you encountered with Mrs. Dobie and some of the other council members could have been managed or even avoided completely if a charter had been in place to guide everyone's behavior."

"But the parish council is already formed," Frank said. "It may be too late."

"Just tell them that your arrival changes things and you want to minimize confusion and the potential for conflict going forward. The best way to do that is to create a new charter that addresses how they'll work together. That way you'll know what to expect from them, and they'll know what to expect from you and from each other."

"What if they think I'm trying to railroad them or ask them to do something they don't want to do?"

"Explain to them that this is what many groups or teams in organizations do if they want to be effective," Charles said.

"Is it? The scariest part of all this is that I've never led anyone through anything like this before. Nor have I even participated in anything like this before. They're going to ask questions or start acting up, and I won't know what to say or do."

"I think they'll probably appreciate what you're trying to do and will be supportive."

"But what do I do if they're not? What happens if they challenge me? I can't defend all this the way you can because I've never done any of it before, and I don't know all the theories and arguments."

"Charles?" Kate interjected. "Why don't you facilitate the team chartering session for Father Frank and the parish council? That way they can all learn from you, and the pressure won't all be on Father Frank to make sure everything works out OK."

"Can you do that?" Frank asked.

"If you want," Charles said. "I've done enough of these kinds of sessions with a large number of groups."

"I'd feel a lot better about things starting out on the right foot if you'd do this for us."

"Don't forget, though, that this is only part of it," said Charles.

"What's the other part?" Frank asked.

"Getting things started in the organizational context, remember?"

"Right. So how do we do that?"

"It's going to be a bit tricky, since the wheels are already rolling at St. Joseph's, so to speak."

"What do you mean?"

"If you were starting the parish from scratch," Charles said, "the first thing you would do is create a vision for what you wanted the parish to be. Then you'd form and charter the parish council in such a way that it would be clear from the beginning that everything the council did would be in support of and within the boundaries of the parish vision."

Frank shook his head. "I'm not sure we have a parish vision."

"I'm certain Monsignor Firko had some sort of vision—at least in his own mind—about where he wanted the parish to go, or there wouldn't be as many good things happening at the parish as there are. But some of the frustrations you experienced exist because not everyone shared that vision. It appears his wasn't a commonly held vision that guided everyone's actions. Otherwise there wouldn't be so much confusion and apparent chaos among the existing council."

"Who develops the vision—the pastor or the parishioners?"

"It can be either or both," Charles replied. "The key isn't so much who develops it. The key factor regarding vision is whether everyone in the parish understands it and fully supports it. It has to be commonly held and supported by all in order to be meaningful. Obviously, the more people there are involved in creating it, the easier it will likely be to get more people to buy into it. Assuming of course, it's clear, compelling, and relevant."

"So if Monsignor Firko was the keeper of the vision for St. Joseph's and he took it with him, what do we do now?" Frank asked.

"That's the catch. The best approach would be for you and the members of the parish council to develop a new vision, but they're not working well together. It doesn't make sense to ask them to start by developing a parish vision because there's a high risk that they will develop one that's not very good. Therefore, the best place to start is by laying the foundation for them to work more effectively together. Then, after they've shown they can do this, you can work with them to create a new and vibrant vision for the parish."

"Now I *know* I'm not going to be able to get through this without your help."

"We'll do this in phases. First we'll have you create a 'first draft' vision for the parish on your own. Using that as a guiding framework, we'll then develop a clear charter for the parish council. Once the team charter is finished for the parish council, we'll then revisit your initial vision for the parish and revise it to create a final version that everyone will share."

Frank shook his head. "I don't have a clue as to what the parish vision should look like."

"It should have five elements," Charles said. "Think of it as five paragraphs, although some may be only a sentence and some of the paragraphs may contain a list of bullet points. The five paragraphs include: a statement of context; a definition of mission or purpose; a statement of values; a description of differentiators that make the parish unique; and a listing of factors that might affect the future of the parish."

"Wait a minute." Frank hurriedly captured the items in his notepad. On a separate page he wrote:

Elements of Parish Vision
1. Statement of context
2. Definition of mission or purpose
3. Statement of values
4. Description of differentiators that make parish unique
5. List of factors that could affect the future

"Can you explain these to me? I'm not sure I understand what each of them means."

"Sure. The statement of context describes the parish and its relationship to its surroundings. For example, it might say something like 'St. Joseph's Parish is one of seventy parishes in the diocese. Located in the neighborhood community of Pine Valley, the parish serves approximately 1,700 middle-income families.'

Yours will be more detailed and comprehensive, but you get the idea."

"So context is more or less a physical description of the parish make-up and how it fits into the broader scheme of things," Frank said.

"That's right. It's the paragraph containing the information that answers the 'what is it?' question. The next paragraph—the purpose or mission element—is a little harder to create. It answers the 'why does it exist?' question."

"OK." Frank added more notes to his list.

"The third paragraph then makes explicit the values you expect to be reflected in everything the parish does," Charles said.

"Wouldn't that be obvious in a parish? I mean, certainly we would want to reflect Christian values."

"But which of those need to be explicit so that people are reminded of them continuously? For example, in one parish Kate and I belonged to years ago, the lay staff had adopted a universally arrogant attitude toward the parishioners. The entire staff had all forgotten that they were there to serve the parishioners. They had lost sight of the fact that service was a value by which they should live. Because they didn't value service, they acted like they were doing the parishioners a favor every time one of us asked for something. They chased a lot of people away from the parish, and maybe even the Church for that matter."

"I can think of a number of values that should serve as guidelines for anyone who works in a parish," Frank said.

"Then the fourth paragraph of the vision statement delineates the factors or characteristics that make the parish unique. It addresses the 'what makes us special or different?' question."

"For example?" Frank furiously continued to take notes. "I thought all parishes are basically the same."

Charles nodded. "In some respects they are. But they all have differences. It's important for everyone— especially those in leadership roles—to know and understand the differences. For example, you know Father Mike Farguson, don't you?"

"I do."

"His first parish was in Salida, Colorado."

"I remember."

"Well, Salida was a community that was on the decline when he took over. The economic condition of the area was depressed. Most of the young families had either moved away or were in the process of moving to places where they could find a better living for their families. I'd guess the average age of his parishioners was well over 60."

"I agree," Frank said.

"Then Father Mike was transferred into a parish in a major suburb of Colorado Springs. The majority of his new parish was young families with kids. A lot of them lived in brand-new homes. Those who didn't lived in neighborhoods that were revitalizing. The needs and make-up of that parish were dramatically different than those of the Salida parish."

"Very much."

"Therefore the vision for each parish would have to be different as well," Charles continued. "It's important to be precise in delineating those differences so everyone knows exactly why certain decisions are made. A lot of times people move into a new parish and never understand why things need to be different from the way they were at their last parish. For example, you'd never consider building a new school unless things changed drastically in Salida. But a school might be a top priority at Father Mike's new parish."

"Isn't that pretty much obvious?" Frank asked.

"That specific example is," Charles replied. "I think you'll find most differences between parishes won't be that dramatic, but it's equally as important to understand them so you and your staff can make the best decisions possible for your current parish."

"That leaves the final paragraph of the vision statement. The one about future factors."

"Right. Let's say your parish anticipates an influx of Hispanic members. Or you definitely see the need for a school in the future. Or you might anticipate other changes in the parish or its environment. You want to state those so everyone is aware they are coming or at least anticipated on some level in the future."

"So these would be major events or changes that could have significant impact on the parish, either from within or externally, that haven't happened yet but are likely to happen at some time in the future."

"Absolutely," Charles nodded. It was obvious he enjoyed working with Frank.

"This is work," Frank said.

"It seems like a lot of work because it's all new to you. But once you get into it, if you do it right, it won't seem like much at all. In fact, it may not even seem like work. Because it will help you clarify your calling in relationship to your new parish, the whole process should be rewarding and fulfilling."

"OK," Frank said. "So where do we go from here?"

Charles looked at his watch. "We take a break."

Frank checked the time. "Wow! I didn't realize what time it is."

"How about Mass? Then we'll have some dinner and take a walk. There's supposed to be a full moon tonight, so it should be a nice evening to get close to nature."

"Great."

Frank scurried out to his car and ferried his things up to his room.

After Mass and dinner they changed into their hiking shoes, gathered some flashlights and jackets, and set out into the brisk mountain air.

"Let's go this way," Charles indicated a trail that led away from the meadow and toward a ridgeline that Frank hadn't visited before.

"Here comes the moon." Kate paused at the top of the first rise in the trail. "Let's watch it come up."

They carefully veered off the trail toward a rock formation about 30 feet away. In the distance toward the east an eerie glow backlit the farthest mountain ridgeline, lighting the surrounding sky like a huge bonfire only God could have ignited.

They watched in silence as the huge, fiery-orange moon barely peeked over the ridgeline, revealing a mere sliver of its full glory. Then proudly, majestically, it rose, virtually unstoppable in a ritual that had repeated itself for countless millennia. *But never more beautiful or dignified than this,* Frank thought. *And this is only one of God's many wonders.*

"Wouldn't it be great if everyone could see and appreciate God's splendors all the time?" he asked.

"That's one of the things we like most about the ranch," Kate said. "Every time we leave here, we take away a renewed sense of appreciation for all of God's creation and blessings."

The color of the moon changed from orange to white as it continued its ascent, and the three slowly made their way back to the trail. The moon's glow was so bright in the thin mountain air that it almost seemed like daylight. They could easily see their shadows dancing alongside them as they continued their evening trek.

At the top of the next hill they came to a large, elongated rock that resembled the back of an 80-foot whale breaching the surface of the ocean as it cruised along some moonlit sea.

"That's a neat formation," Frank said.

Charles nodded. "Wait 'til you see what's on the other side. Cardinal Eggleston discovered it when he was hiking around up here a couple of years ago."

They hastened their steps. Just as they rounded the head of the rock a long, deep *wooing* sound pierced the night and filled the air around them. The suddenness, combined with the strength of the call, made them freeze in their tracks. The hair stood up on the back of Frank's neck, sending chills down his spine.

"Owl," Charles said. "Probably a great horned owl in that stand of pines to the left of the meadow. We might get a glimpse of him if he decides to take off. I don't know if he will, though. He doesn't seem too intimidated by us so far."

As Frank's pulse slowed to normal, the trio resumed their foray along the opposite side of the rock to about its middle.

"Here we are," Charles said, sounding as if he'd just revealed the Holy Grail.

Frank said nothing. He didn't want to appear as though he'd missed anything important, but at the same time he didn't know what it was he should be seeing. This side of the whale-shaped rock seemed pretty much like the other side: all granite, worn smooth by the forces of nature over the years. Some spots were more eroded than others, creating pock marks or depressions here and there, but that was about it.

Frank noticed a ten-foot-long bulge near where they stood. The bulge resembled a fin that extended down into the water from the whale's mid-section. Along the outer edge of the bulge a couple of feet from the ground, the wind and rain had gouged out a deep depression in the shape of a small barrel that had been split in half vertically. A few inches up on either side, the edges turned outward horizontally, then continued up until blending back into the rock with almost perfect symmetry.

"*This* is Cardinal Eggleston's discovery," Charles said.

"The rock?"

"No, the seat."

"Seat?"

"Yes. This seat. He calls it the Seat of Heavenly Thoughts."

Charles ran his hand back and forth across the bottom of the eroded depression. "Let me show you."

He turned and sat in the depression, fitting perfectly. "Replete with arm rests and all. Now you try it." He stood and offered the seat to Frank, who took his place.

"This is surprisingly comfortable," he said.

Charles nodded. "You'd never know you were sitting on a rock, would you? And the most amazing thing about it is that everyone, regardless of size or shape, says the rock fits them perfectly. Dozens of people have sat there and they all say it feels like it was designed just for them."

"Add me to the list," Frank said. "I can't imagine a chair feeling more comfortable than this."

"Good. Now, tomorrow morning I have a few business tasks. So, I want you to find your way back here and create a first draft of what you think the vision statement might look like for St. Joseph's Parish. I want it to be as good as you can make it—but realize that later on, after we've chartered the parish council and you've learned a bit more about the parish and its needs, we'll finalize it. The purpose of this draft is merely to give us enough focus to make it through the chartering process with the parish council."

"I'll give it a try."

"You'll do just fine," Kate said.

They made their way back down the trail to the cabin. After completing Evening Prayer together, they turned in for the night. Frank's mind was filled with all sorts of ideas and possibilities as he finally drifted off to sleep.

The next morning, they celebrated Mass in the chapel, then had breakfast before Frank took off for the Seat of Heavenly Thoughts and Charles retreated to his office. Kate had a few errands to run in town.

Once again Frank found himself almost floating through the tall pines as he eagerly looked forward to his assignment. He reached the whale-shaped rock and immediately plopped down into the Seat of Heavenly Thoughts with notepad and pencil in hand.

Even though he had thought of almost nothing other than his potential vision statement since their visit here the night before, he decided it would be best if he collected his thoughts a bit more before he actually wrote anything down on paper. So he said a short prayer of thanks to God for giving him the support he needed to fulfill his calling and asked for His continued guidance as he moved forward. Then he leaned back, closed his eyes, and meditated.

It occurred to him that most of the possibilities he could think of for the parish could be grouped into four categories. The first category was that of evangelization. In his mind this meant reaching out to potential new Catholics in the community and also doing something to bring fallen-away Catholics back into the fold. He had no idea whether the current evangelization efforts fit the community, or even more important, whether there were any activities even happening. He had seen some things on paper, but if it was like his last parish, that's where it ended. It was more of a program on paper than something people actually did.

The second category of outcomes would be that of the sacraments. He asked himself, *Do the parishioners participate in the sacraments in an engaged manner? Do they have a strong understanding of Catholic theology?* He didn't feel bad answering "No" to the questions because, he surmised, most parishioners in most parishes seem to be fairly apathetic. *But where are the biggest gaps?* he asked himself, thinking that his vision would close the most important of those gaps.

He surmised that his third category would be catechesis. He wondered, *Are parishioners learning as much as possible about our faith and the teachings of Jesus Christ? If not, where should we put the emphasis on making it better?* This raised issues about the kind of religious education programs, youth ministries, and adult programs they should try to develop, and whether they should build a school. He heard there had been talk of that buzzing around the parish for years.

The final category was service. He had been told that the Christian Family Movement members in the parish went into a nearby low-income neighborhood and fixed up some needy family's home once a year. He was sure the parishioners probably had a toy drive for poor kids at Christmas and maybe did some other seasonal things. But beyond that, he wasn't really sure what else was happening.

As Frank opened his eyes to start recording his thoughts in his notepad, he noticed a doe and her fawn in the meadow. The mother was peacefully grazing as the spotted fawn played awkwardly around her, chasing an odd butterfly here and there and exploring the different flowers that bloomed in the morning sun.

The doe looked up at him and froze for a moment as Frank slowly turned to a blank page. Once she realized he was staying where he was and doing his own thing, she casually resumed her grazing.

The scene reminded Frank of something he had read and then memorized in high school. He replayed the words in his mind as he had done at least a thousand times before.

> *A man whispered, "God, speak to me."*
> *And a meadowlark sang,*
> *But the man did not hear.*
> *So the man yelled, "God, speak to me."*
> *And thunder rolled across the sky,*
> *But the man did not listen.*

The man looked around and said, "God, let me see you."
And a star shined brightly,
But the man did not notice.
And the man shouted, "God, show me a miracle!"
And a life was born,
But the man did not know.
So the man cried out in despair, "Touch me, God,
and let me know you are here!"
Whereupon God reached down and touched the man,
But the man brushed away the butterfly and walked on.

— Author unknown

As Frank reflected on these words, a powerful feeling overwhelmed him. It was even more intense than those he had experienced at the shrine of the three shepherds and the Angel of Peace at Loca do Cabeco in Fatima, if that were possible. Once again he felt as though his entire being radiated with a grace so pure that he could have disintegrated into the world around him.

God is present in me as a leader, too! he thought. *I always put myself in God's presence when I pray and I certainly recognize His presence in the Eucharist, but I've been less diligent in doing the same when I carry out the day-to-day activities of running the parish.* With a flood of emotion he suddenly realized he was developing an entirely new appreciation for God's statement to Moses in the book of Exodus: "Fear not, for I shall be with you."

Maybe if He had said, 'I shall be within you as you fulfill all your pastoral duties' I would have caught on sooner, he thought.

Good leader, good shepherd, he reflected. *The two are one. Leadership isn't something separate from my pastoral duties. It isn't something I can opt to do instead of or in addition to being a good shepherd. Rather it's an integral part of all I do. It's what enables me to govern, sanctify, and educate to the fullest of my God-given potential. It's a means to those ends, but a means that can't be separate from those ends if I am to completely fulfill them.*

Good leader, good shepherd, he thought again, as he continued to reflect on all that meant to him and to his calling. *I think I finally get it.*

Quite some time passed before he emerged from his reverie and returned his focus to his notepad. He wrote the four categories—sacraments, catechesis, evangelization, and service—as titles across the tops of four consecutive pages. Then, underneath the titles he divided the remainder of the pages into two vertical columns. At the top of each of the four left-hand columns he wrote, "Questions to answer." Then he labeled each right-hand column, "Items to consider." Then he began to fill in both columns on each of the four pages. This took a while because he paused often to think and reflect as he flipped back and forth between the pages.

Filling out the pages was both energizing and taxing. It was energizing because thinking about all the opportunities and challenges he would face as pastor was exciting. He never before realized how much potential there was to make a difference for people. But it was taxing because it was the first time he had ever thought in terms of outcomes. Always in the past when he thought of performing his priestly duties it had been just that–*performing duties*. In other words, he had thought of his priestly duties more along the lines of activities he needed to do or tasks he needed to perform. To think of his duties now in the context of producing outcomes with and for people added an entirely new dimension he had never before considered. He liked it, and it made all the sense in the world. It was just different and, therefore, mentally taxing.

Soon he ran out of writing room on the pages he had prepared, so he flipped the pages, divided the back of each into two columns, and began filling them out as well.

He was just starting to run out of ideas when he heard Charles making his way around the head of the whale rock. He looked up at Charles then quickly glanced at his watch, surprised to see that it was already noon. It didn't seem possible that he had spent the entire morning here. The time had flown by. He glanced at the meadow and noticed the doe and her fawn were long gone.

"How's it going?" Charles asked.

"Far better than I thought it would. But I think I've generated way more questions than answers."

"Good." Charles nodded knowingly.

"I was hoping I'd have a completed first draft of my vision statement this morning. I need to answer a lot of questions I hadn't even thought about until this morning, then it's going to take some work after that."

"Great. Show me what you've done."

Frank shared with Charles the insights he had gained about how his leadership responsibilities related to and supported his pastoral duties. He also shared with him the changes he had made in the way he started thinking about outcomes versus mere activity as he anticipated fulfilling his pastoral role. Finally, he told Charles about the four areas of outcomes he had deduced as patterns from all the questions and issues he had wrestled with all morning. He concluded by showing Charles the pages of questions and concerns he had compiled in each of the four categories.

"That's a lot of thinking for one morning," Charles said.

Frank nodded. "The morning went by in a hurry. But I don't know if I'm closer to or farther away from where I'm supposed to be."

"You've made a lot of progress. It's just that before now, you didn't know how far you needed to go. Ignorance was bliss," Charles said. "Now you understand what you need to know to get you where you need to be. Understanding the gap between where you are and where you want to be sometimes creates a bit of tension. But you need to realize that it's a healthy tension—you're a lot closer to where you need to be than you were when you didn't know any better."

"OK." Frank reflected on this new insight. Charles' comment about ignorance being bliss struck a particularly resonant chord. He immediately thought of several priests he had observed in the past who had either ignored or not recognized different problems existing in their parishes. Frank had never understood why they were so comfortable not addressing these issues, which obviously had an adverse impact in their parishes. *They didn't know any better,* he thought. *Ignorance was bliss.* Right then and there he made a vow not to be complacent with his own ignorance ever again.

"Here. I brought us some lunch." Charles slung his backpack around and unzipped the top. He handed Frank a tuna sandwich, a plastic bag filled with carrot sticks, and a bottle of water. Frank gave thanks and blessed the food before they started eating.

"What are the next steps?" he asked between bites.

"You've already pointed out the most obvious one. You need to go back to St. Joseph's and answer all the questions you've collected, then finalize your draft of the vision."

"I should be able to do that by the end of next week."

"Then we should schedule two meetings fairly close together with the parish council. Tell them I'll be there and the purpose of the two meetings is to create a charter for how we're going to work together in the future."

"I can do that," Frank said.

"At the meeting I'll explain to them about vision and charter. You present the initial draft of your vision, then I'll take them through the chartering process."

"Sounds good."

"Then we'll go back and review, revise if necessary, and adopt the vision," Charles said.

"OK."

"One of the outcomes of the chartering session will be meeting guidelines for the parish council, so I'll attend the first meeting or two just to help facilitate and see that the guidelines are followed. After that you should be off and crawling."

"That's it? That's all there is to it?"

Charles nodded. "That's the end of the beginning. There's a lot more to learn, and many more challenges. But if you get off to a good beginning, it'll make those challenges much easier to face."

"Give me examples of some of the other things I need to learn."

"For starters, we'll need to go back and learn a lot more about leading self and leading others in a one-to-one context."

"I almost forgot about that," Frank said.

"You'll need to make sure that everyone's individual vision for his or her role is in line with the parish vision once it is finalized. Then you'll need to ensure that the initiatives they are pursuing support those personal visions. Finally you'll need to know how to assess everyone's individual performance relative to those initiatives, and give them the support they need to be able to accomplish those initiatives. Once those foundations are in place, it will free up more of your time to focus on your personal pastoral responsibilities."

"I can see that now."

"Don't feel like you need to learn everything at once," Charles said. "First of all, it's impossible. But more important, even if you could, it would be less effective. Learn first things first. Apply what you learn. Then build on that foundation to learn and apply more. See it as a journey, much the same way you see your faith journey. Pick up different competencies as the situations arise where they are needed."

Frank nodded. "Like right now, envisioning in all the contexts is the most important for me because everyone seems to have a different focus. If we can get each to adopt a similar vision we can begin to get people to work together."

"Exactly. Then once you get everyone singing from the same sheet of music, so to speak, you can encourage them to fulfill their callings even better. You'll have less conflict, more cooperation, and much greater fulfillment for everyone, including yourself."

"What about relationships?" Frank asked.

"I think the best approach with relationships is to wait until you've answered this first list of questions you've compiled. My guess is that there's at least one disgruntled organization somewhere in the parish environment. If that's the case, then let's focus on that one first. I'll work through with you the best way to create a positive alliance with whatever organization it is. Then we'll simply prioritize the rest of them from there until all the relationships are clarified and manageable."

"You bring so much order and logic to all this stuff. I can't believe how different it is to hear you talk about it than it has been to see it through my eyes. All I've been able to see is chaos, disorder, and conflict. You make it sound like all that chaos can be turned into peace and harmony almost with the wave of a wand."

"It's not magic," Charles explained. "It's knowing what to do *and then* having the ability and the energy to do it. It's nothing new, though many people think that much of what happens in the realm of leadership as being somehow mysterious. Many of the saints, most of our popes, countless cardinals, bishops, and many clergy have been good leaders. I think we often discount their leadership abilities because we focus so much on their spirituality and holiness as the primary context through which we study their lives. But the great paradox is that many of them could not have projected their holiness to the levels they did were it not for their leadership abilities."

Frank thought, *Good leader, good shepherd.*

"So I'll make you a deal," Charles said.

"What's that?"

"You continue to help me grow spiritually. Guide me toward a better understanding of the teachings of

Christ, and help me learn what I need to learn to be a better Catholic. And in return I'll help you learn the mysteries of leadership in a pastoral setting, which you'll find out aren't really so mysterious after all. But you'll learn them in a way that will free you up to bring your ministry closer to God as well, allowing you to fulfill the full potential of your calling."

"That sounds like a deal worth taking," Frank responded.

They walked back to the cabin together, grateful for what they had learned. They felt the extraordinary grace God had given them through their unique combination of gifts. Their efforts would bring glory and honor to God while touching people's lives and the world in a very special way.

The end of the beginning ...

APPENDIX

A New View of Leadership

Imagine you're on a journey back from outer space. You passed the moon a while ago and are some 50,000 miles away from Earth. The jewel that glows in the thickness of night is the planet you call home: a small blue ball surrounded by blackness. As your spacecraft hurls through space you begin to see the great divisions of blue oceans and taupe-colored land masses through the cover of clouds and atmosphere.

Now consider your journey as a leader. The first thing you begin to notice are the great divisions of the contexts–SOTOR as seen in Figure 1.

Figure 1: SOTOR—The five contexts of leadership for priests

Obviously, you may not lead in all five contexts all the time. If you are an associate pastor, for example, you may have little opportunity to lead in the Organizational Context. But you should be able to discern the context in which you *are* leading, understand how your context affects or is affected by the others, and adapt your leadership behavior appropriately.

The 1,000-Mile View

As you travel closer to the Earth from outer space, you notice something remarkable. From hundreds of miles away you can start to make out details, such as the Great Wall of China and the Nile River.

So too, in your leadership journey, you become aware of more detail. You can now see five layers of rings that circumvent all the contexts. These rings represent five leadership practices that are relevant regardless of the context you are leading and are shown in Figure 2. These are the practices that define what you *do* as a leader.

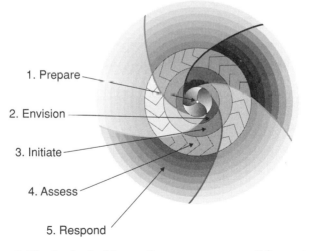

Contextual Leadership™

1. Prepare
2. Envision
3. Initiate
4. Assess
5. Respond

Figure 2: The five leadership practices common across all five contexts

Leadership practices help you in two ways. First, you don't have to reinvent the wheel every time you move from one context to another. The process–to Prepare, Envision, Initiate, Assess, and Respond is the same for each context.

Second, the five practices provide you with a consistent process that *links* the contexts so they don't exist in isolation.

Let's say that you and your parish have adapted Contextual Leadership. After you Prepare for leadership by understanding how your personality influences your leadership behavior, you then Envision. If you begin in the Self–Context, you envision by creating an individual vision specific to your role. That vision gets reinforced when you and your pastor envision in the One-to-One Context–integrating your individual vision into the expectations of your role. In the Team Context, your team envisions by creating a charter that integrates your work-related vision with those of team and alliance members to form a common sense of purpose. In the Organizational Context, envisioning is a top-down and bottom-up effort in which your vision becomes of a greater whole–making the organization's vision that much stronger. No matter how grand an organization's vision sounds, it is only as strong as the individual visions that support it. When you form strategic relationships, you integrate the vision of your organization with another.

The power of a vision increases exponentially when you envision in all five contexts–especially when the energy from the vision is then harnessed through goals that are supported contextually.

Touchdown Approach: Practicing Leadership *within* Each Context

In your journey toward Earth, the closer you get, the more detail you see. Each continent has its own appearance and distinctive qualities. In your leadership journey the more hands-on you become, the more you recognize the distinctive characteristics and demands of each context. So while the process to practicing leadership is the same for all five contexts, you begin to realize that the *application* of those practices is different in each context as shown in Figure 3.

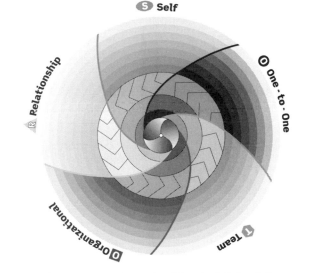

Figure 3: The Contextual Leadership Model for Priests

Notice the added detail to the model—in the "Assess" ring you see the chevrons that represent the five phases of performance; in the "Respond" ring you see the shadings that represent the skills pertinent in each context.

A FINAL METAPHOR

As you are about to touchdown from your remarkable journey, imagine the abrupt shock as you transition from zero gravity to the pull of gravity as you enter the Earth's atmosphere. Things are happening fast and furious, when suddenly you realize that instead of landing in the ocean and bobbing up to be rescued as planned, your spacecraft just keeps going. You find yourself being hurled through the murky depths of the ocean, hitting the ocean floor, and entering the Earth's core in a shocking, bumpy, and uncomfortable ride. Sometimes it's darker than night, sometimes it's so bright you can see every detail hidden in the strata of the Earth's inner layers. At the Earth's core you discover molten lava—unformed, raw, and boiling to the point of pressure, which if not sufficiently released, will explode uncontrollably into the Earth's atmosphere.

Understanding your personality, acknowledging your dispositional patterns, exploring your values, and investigating your persona as you Prepare for leadership can be as rough as the journey to the center of the Earth; it can be an arduous, frightening, and painstaking experience. It can also be a satisfying and fruitful experience. The journey to mastering contextual leadership includes an exploration of your personality and how your disposition, values, and persona affect your leadership behavior. "He who knows others is learned, but he who knows himself is wise."

At the very core is your spirituality. A sound spiritual base provides the essence for everything you do as a leader.

This is why Prepare is the practice at the center of the Contextual Leadership Model. Your leadership begins with who you are spiritually and extends to everyone you lead in each of the five contexts.

Contextual Leadership Grid

We have created a grid that encapsulates the details of Contextual Leadership, shown in Figure 4 on page 120. There is a column for each of the five contexts, beginning from the left with the Self Context. Each row defines how the five leadership practices—Prepare, Envision, Initiate, Assess, and Respond—play out in each context.

Contextual Leadership is how you engage and satisfy the values and needs of the people you lead in an arena of conflict, competition, or achievement that results in them taking action through a mutually shared vision to sustained high performance.

Figure 4: The Contextual Leadership Grid*

Self Context	One-to-One Context	Team Context
Developing the skill set and the mindset to accept responsibility and take the initiative for succeeding in your work-related role	Developing the abilities and focusing the energy of your direct reports so they can attain and sustain independent achievement in their work-related roles	Gathering, structuring, and developing the collective abilities and energies of a team of people with a common purpose, and guiding them to the achievement of interdependent goals and sustained high performance

Organizational Context	**Alliance Context**
Directly and indirectly influencing and aligning individual and team efforts toward fulfillment of the organization's purpose through systems, processes, and structures	Using networks and bilateral relationships to create a third entity that extends beyond corporate boundaries and achieves the goals and serves the mutual interests of all the members of the alliance

	Self Context	One-to-One Context
Prepare Recognizing, controlling, and adapting your disposition-driven behavior; developing personal values; and investigating your persona, so your leadership behavior does not predispose you to act in ways that may sabotage your effectiveness.	Prepare by reconciling your disposition-driven and values-motivated behavior with the expectations of your work-related role, vision, and goals.	Prepare by reconciling your disposition-driven and values-motivated behavior as a means of leading people who report to you as they fulfill their work-related visions and organizational initiatives.

Team Context	Organizational Context	Alliance Context
Prepare by reconciling your disposition-driven and values-motivated behavior as a means of leading your team as it fulfills its charter.	Prepare by reconciling your disposition-driven and values-motivated behavior as a means of leading your organization as it fulfills its vision and achieves its initiatives.	Prepare by reconciling your disposition-driven and values-motivated behavior as a means of leading your alliance to fulfill its "big idea."

	Self Context	One-to-One Context
Envision Visualizing an inspirational ideal one can aspire to, crafting a statement of purpose one can be dedicated to, proclaiming rank-ordered values that act as a noble guide for behavior and decision making, and aligning the vision across contexts.	Envision by creating a motivating vision for your work-related role that integrates with your personal vision, helps you sustain enthusiasm for your role, and aligns with both your manager's expectations and the organization's vision.	Envision by guiding those who report to you to generate a compelling vision of their work-related role that imbues their role with meaning and gives life to the organization's vision.

Team Context	Organizational Context	Alliance Context
Envision by designing a blueprint for the team that will inspire and mobilize the team members as they initiate their charter, and that aligns with the organization's vision and expectations.	Envision by establishing an inspiring vision for the organization that becomes a unifying force, informing strategic planning and ultimately acting as a noble guide for people's behavior and decision making.	Envision by developing a stimulating vision for the alliance that capitalizes on the synergy that comes from discovering a common purpose out of the disparate and potentially conflicting agendas of alliance members.

	Self Context	One-to-One Context
Initiate Establishing and facilitating the goals, expectations, ground rules, operating guidelines, and steps for implementation that embody, enable, foster, and sustain a work-related vision.	Initiate by creating a personal performance plan that defines Key Responsibility Areas, SMART goals, and action steps for his or her achievement that are aligned with your work-related vision and the organization's.	Initiate by establishing performance objectives based on Key Responsibility Areas, SMART goals, and a development plan for your direct report that is aligned with the direct report's work-related vision as well as the organization's goals and vision.

Team Context	Organizational Context	Alliance Context
Initiate by establishing a high-impact team charter that is aligned with the sponsor's vision for the team and includes team member-generated vision, purpose, values, goals, and operating principles.	Initiate by outlining a strategy supported by initiatives with action steps for their achievement that are aligned with the organizational vision.	Initiate by establishing a charter outlining the alliance's major goals and operating principles for fulfilling the alliance's "big idea," as well as the visions of the partners in the strategic relationship.

	Self Context	**One-to-One Context**
Assess Appraising the Ability and Energy of an individual, team, organization, or alliance to achieve a specific outcome.	Assess your own phase of performance by looking at indicators of Ability and Energy on a work-related goal.	Assess your direct report's phase of performance by looking at indicators of Ability and Energy related to an agreed upon goal or task.

Team Context	Organizational Context	Alliance Context
Assess the team's phase of performance by looking at indicators of Ability and Energy related to goals and outcomes identified in the team charter.	Assess the organization's phase of performance by looking at indicators of Ability and Energy of the people in the organization as they implement an organizational initiative.	Assess the alliance's phase of performance by looking at indicators of Energy and Ability related to the goals and outcomes identified in the alliance charter.

	Self Context	One-to-One Context
Respond Taking the appropriate leadership action with individuals, teams, organizations, or alliances to develop their abilities and energies to achieve specific outcomes.	Respond by using the skills to: Sustain Self Motivation, DISCover Time, Solicit and Receive Feedback, Promote Your Solutions, and Practice Menteeship to get the focus and inspiration you need based on your phase of performance for a particular goal.	Respond by using the skills to: Show How, Proactively Listen, Facilitate Problem Solving, Give Effective Feedback, and DISCover Others to give your direct report the focusing and inspiring needed based on his or her current phase of performance on a particular goal.

Team Context	Organizational Context	Alliance Context
Respond by using the skills to give your team the focus and inspiration needed based on its current phase of performance on a particular goal: Structure Meetings, Facilitate Group Problem Solving, Assess Team Process, DISCover Group Dynamics, and Resolve Conflict.	Respond by using the skills to: Scan the Environment, Frame a Compelling Message, Manage Organizational Problem Solving, Promote Justice, and Celebrate Success to provide people in the organization the focus and inspiration needed based on their collective phase of performance on an organizational initiative.	Respond by using the skills to: Conceptualize and Form the Alliance, Facilitate Non-Adversarial Problem Solving, and Prepare for Win-Win Negotiations to give the alliance the focus and inspiration needed based on its current phase of performance on a particular goal.

*Adapted from Chapter 35 of *Contextual Leadership*, published by Financial Times, Prentice Hall, 2007.

About the Authors

Dr. Dick Lyles is a co-developer of the Good Leaders, Good Shepherds leadership development program for Catholic priests offered by the Catholic Leadership Institute (CLI). He is the CEO of Leadership Legacies, a company that focuses on developing a new generation of leaders. Lyles co-founded Maric College in San Diego, served as president of The Ken Blanchard Companies®, and currently sits on the board of directors for a number of firms. His best-selling books include *Winning Ways: Four Secrets for Getting Great Results by Working Well with People.*

Tim Flanagan is the founder and chairman of the Catholic Leadership Institute. A graduate of Villanova University with a degree in economics, Tim's professional career has spanned over thirty-eight years in the financial services industry. Tim has been trained by The Center for Creative Leadership, the American Management Association Leadership Program, Stephen Covey's Principle Centered Leadership Institute, and Pecos River Learning Center. In 2003, he was awarded the designation of Chartered Leadership Fellow by the American College.

Dr. Drea Zigarmi is a founding associate of the Ken Blanchard Companies and co-creator of *Situational Leadership® II*, today's best-of-class developmental leadership model. He co-authored the two-million-copy bestseller *Leadership and the One Minute Manager* and, most recently, *The Leader Within.* Dr. Zigarmi is a co-developer of Catholic Leadership Institute's Good Leaders, Good Shepherds leadership development program for Catholic priests.

Susan Fowler, a co-developer of the Good Leaders, Good Shepherds leadership development program, is one of the world's foremost experts on personal empowerment. She is creator and lead developer of the Ken Blanchard Companies' Situational Self Leadership, today's best-of-class self-leadership and personal empowerment program. Fowler's publications include *The Team Leader's Idea-a-Day Guide* (with Drea Zigarmi), *Empowerment* (with Ken Blanchard), and *Self Leadership and the One Minute Manager* (with Ken Blanchard and Laurence Hawkins).

CATHOLIC LEADERSHIP INSTITUTE

About Catholic Leadership Institute

Founded in 1991, Catholic Leadership Institute (CLI) is a non-profit lay association of the faithful whose mission is to build Catholic leaders for today and tomorrow. CLI has helped over 9,000 individuals which includes priests, seminarians, lay, religious, young adult, and campus leaders to discover their mission in life and fulfill their God-given potential.

Catholic Leadership Institute combines the science of leadership with the wisdom of Jesus Christ and the Catholic Church.

CLI is based in the Philadelphia area. More information about the Catholic Leadership Institute is available by emailing info@CatholicLeaders.org or by visiting www.CatholicLeaders.org.

Good Leaders, Good Shepherds

Catholic Leadership Institute is partnering with dioceses nationwide to offer Good Leaders, Good Shepherds: a two-year, clergy leadership development curriculum designed specifically for the priest as pastor. The program trains priests in five key contexts of leadership: leadership of self, leadership in a one-to-one context, leadership of teams, leadership of an organization, leadership of strategic relationships.

Additionally, Catholic Leadership Institute provides leadership development opportunities to lay adults and parish staff to empower them to maximize their potential as Catholic leaders in their families, workplaces, communties and Church.

Ascension Press is the publisher of popular Catholic books and adult faith formation resources including the renowned *Great Adventure Bible Timeline* and parish-based programs on the Theology of the Body. For more information, call 1-800-376-0520 or visit www.AscensionPress.com